T0247027

ANY GIRL

a novel

Caroline van Rooyen

We acknowledge the support of the Canada Council for the Arts for our publishing program. We also acknowledge support from the Government of Ontario through the Ontario Arts Council, and the support of the Government of Canada through the Canada Book Fund.

Cover design by Sabrina Pignataro
Cover photos: stevenfoley / Profile Silhouettes – Women stock illustration / iStockphoto.com

Library and Archives Canada Cataloguing in Publication

Title: Any girl : a novel / Caroline van Rooyen.
Names: Van Rooyen, Caroline, author.
Identifiers: Canadiana (print) 20220191719 | Canadiana (ebook) 20220191727 | ISBN 9781774150634
    (softcover) | ISBN 9781774150641 (EPUB) | ISBN 9781774150658 (PDF)
Classification: LCC PS8643.A565 A79 2022 | DDC jC813/.6—dc23

Printed and bound in Canada by Coach House Printing

Mawenzi House Publishers Ltd.
39 Woburn Avenue (B)
Toronto, Ontario M5M 1K5
Canada
www.mawenzihouse.com

To S and Z
Thank you for your constant support

1. A THREATENING NOTE

A TIGHTLY FOLDED NOTE lands on my desk. Annoyed, I flick it to the floor and kick it behind me. Trigger happy Mrs Horack is teaching and I don't want a Friday detention. Within seconds the note reappears on my desk like a persistent fly—which raises the question: why is someone bugging me right now, demanding my immediate attention? Of course my mind flips back to last Friday, like a tongue finding the gap left by an extracted tooth, and my fingers tremble as I unfold the note and read.

Now you die.

I freeze, feel the glare of a spotlight placing me centre stage: this is a joke, isn't it? I glance across the room at the usual clowns, the rugby boys, and try to catch the eye of their leader, David McNeil, to say he's gone too far, but he has his head down on his desk with his eyes closed. If this was his set-up he'd be watching for my outrage or scared reaction, ready to lead the mocking laughter. Acid bile starts to rise up my throat as fear digs its sharp nails into my flesh. No! Don't go there. They don't know what happened. I study each member of that team, all fake sleeping until, hesitantly, I reach the last desk in that row.

Kevin Abbott sits low in his chair, hands thrust deep into his trouser pockets, eyes closed. Like a snake hiding in the grass, sensing my gaze he looks up at me, raises one eyebrow, winks slowly, then settles back down. He's not a pretty snake. His cheeks are a rash of white zits, his mouse-brown hair is lank.

Fortunately for him two cold sores prove that he has lips.

Terror sweat re-ignites the scorching net of cigarette burns and cuts that cover my body. I know it was Kevin who wrote the note. That makes the threat real. Kevin rigs drugs for Travis Richter. Travis Richter leads the school's criminal gang, selling drugs, stolen goods and even examination papers. Last Friday night, Richter's boys tossed me into the hands of a rapist.

I can smell the cigarette smoke, feel my flesh burning, and hear the words, "You're picking them young. This one's what, ten?" "No, an undersized fifteen." They laugh; the short, harsh yips of wild dogs encircling a kill.

I was a child. Last Friday I was a child.

I'm shaking so badly my teeth clatter and click like cheap grandma dentures. I scan the door. Is it already too late? Are they out there waiting for me? How do they intend to do it, a knife, a bullet, or a shove over the balcony? I have to leave now. Legally, I can't just get up and walk out of the school. I need a Permission Slip from the office. The office is a staircase and two quads away. That's a long time to be a target. I can go AWOL, but if the school finds out they'll report me to Child Welfare. Mom and I don't want Child Welfare sniffing at our door, not now.

"Hey! July, bell's gone!"

I nearly wet myself. Johnny Dunst looms over me, all muscle and blond buzz-cut, smelling faintly of soap and sweat. He plays prop for the under-sixteen rugby team and is the size of a barn door and a little less smart.

What is he doing at my desk? Is he my killer? I scoot up against the wall. This doesn't get me far enough away. Why him? He never speaks to me. We aren't friends.

"Want help?" he asks, stepping closer and reaching for my bag.

"No! Don't touch me. Stay away!" With hands the size of

oven gloves, he could snap my neck like a twig.

"Will you two please leave?" Mrs Horack calls from the front of the class. "My grade twelve group will be arriving any minute. And you'll be late for your next class."

"Yes ma'am, right away ma'am." I stand up, forgetting to brace myself for the wave of pain that crashes across my body as my wounds pull, rip, and bleed. All the air is sucked out of my lungs. As I lean heavily on my desk, swirls and webs twist and glide across my vision.

I'm broken. How can I fight? I need a hospital, not a battlefield.

Mrs Horack says, "If you don't leave now, I will send you both to the office."

"That's where I'm going. I'm sick," I reply, stuffing my books into my bag, which I then use as a shield to push back Johnny. "Out the way, Johnny, I need to leave." I'm a Yorkshire Terrier attempting to shove a Saint Bernard: unless it wants to move it won't. Pan-faced, he takes my bag out of my hands and slings it over his shoulder.

"I'll take you." He heads for the door.

Do I trust him? He's not my friend, but he's not my enemy. General opinion is that he's too lazy to be mean. Does laziness also make you trustworthy? His father is a pastor. Why did that come to my mind? Nice parents can generate thugs. He's a classmate, time is short, and I need help. I follow him out the door.

He calls to his friends, who are waiting outside. "Hey, David, tell van Zyl I've taken July to the office." A roar of laughter erupts.

"Sure, okay," David McNeil replies. "I'll give him your message. It won't help you survive if you don't bring a late note." David goes off, taking his group with him. Comments float back.

"Johnny's slumming it."

"Wants chips not caviar."

Johnny ignores them and looks back at me as if to say, "Come on, time is money."

He makes a great bodyguard: silent and focussed. No chit-chat. Slower traffic bulldozed out of the way.

Those foolish enough to consider us a newly formed Johnny-July duo will surely judge it a serious lack of judgement on his part. It is, because now Richter will train his sights on Johnny. Then again with all the school's rugby teams on Johnny's side, maybe it isn't even an issue for him. I'm alone and my thoughts are swirling freely in my mind. Does Johnny work for Richter? Why would he? Richter sells drugs. Johnny doesn't do drugs; he's as innocent as a new-born hippo. So why is this giant helping me? Someone is pulling his strings. Will he demand a security payment from me? The only deal I'll make will be in cash. I have money, but not on me right now.

We pass through the tunnel into the east quad and then slow down. In this quad with its staff room, the principal's office, and the administrative offices, an adult is always watching. I feel safer already.

At the office door Johnny gives me my bag and leaves. It's like he had a job to do and he did it. I'm confused and grateful. Pushing open the door, I head for the counter, determined to get permission to go home, where I know I'll be safe. I want to stay alive.

2. THE KEYS

"WHAT'S THE MATTER, JULY, you're very pale!" Mrs Prince says, walking up towards me. I like her. She looks me in the eye as if I matter. My mom does that.

"My skull is about to explode. It feels like there's a crazy rabbit trying to kick its way out. Please, may I go home?" To make my point, I push my fingers into the soft indentations just above my ears. It feels good. When I get home I will put a hot cloth across my forehead.

Mrs Prince picks up the phone. "I'll call your mom. It's probably the flu. Did you have your flu shot?" She waves the phone at me. "No one is answering."

"She won't. My mom's a nurse. She can't get to her phone. I take the bus home. They run every ten minutes down Lynwood Road. I'll be fine. Oh, and yes, I had my flu shot." I lean on the counter and run my fingers up through my thick brown hair, making it stand straight up. If looking pathetic earns me a ticket home, I win.

"Sorry, dear. Rules say your parent or legal guardian has to collect you. Why don't you lie down in the sickroom?" Mrs Prince picks up a set of keys. All my plans slide sideways.

"No! Please, I just want to go home. There's a bus in ten minutes. Could you ask Mr McNeil? I feel horrible."

Mrs Prince pats my hand. "That's why you need to lie down before you fall down. What if you keel over in the bus? Who will help you? I'll ask Mr McNeil as soon as he's free." She reaches under the counter for a packet of headache tablets and hands me two and a bottle of water. "Take these for now. Keep the bottle. I'll take you up. You look dead on your feet."

I have to play along. Try again later. I don't want her tracking down my mother. Slipping the stapler from the counter into my pocket, I follow. I need a weapon and it qualifies. If Richter sees me go up to the sickroom I will be dead on my feet.

The sickroom occupies the space above the home economics centre.

"All these security gates even up here," Mrs Prince says, unlocking the door. "Do you know, criminals will take the tiles off a roof and climb in that way? They steal computers, stoves, anything. They broke into North Lodge over at Girls' High last year, while the girls were sleeping." She shivers at the horror. "You may switch on the bar heater, but keep it away from the bedding. We don't want a fire. You climb into bed. I'll come back when I have news." She leaves, closing the door behind her.

I count slowly back from thirty, then ease open the door and remove the key from the lock. With the rest of the bunch, I now have in my hand the keys to the entire school, proof that the universe still wants me alive! Why else would it hand me the keys to my own fortress? No one uses the school at night. If my flat becomes unsafe, I can hunker down here for a couple of nights, disappear off the grid, and figure out my next move. You can't kill what you can't find, can you? Feeling encouraged I put the keys into my bag.

To make sure Mrs Prince doesn't miss her keys, I leave the door unlocked. Then I drag a chair in front of the door, wrap myself in the duvet, and sit down with the open stapler in my hand. Shooting two staples at the garbage bin reveals that the stapler is useless as a weapon, unless I got close enough to whack him in the face with it. I need a real weapon. Not a gun, they're noisy. A knife, small enough to fit inside my school blazer pocket, sharp enough to slice raw flesh, and strong enough to change the outcome of a fight. From now on I will defend myself.

The room warms. The medication kicks in. I'm almost asleep when the door opens. I rocket up from the chair like a lit fire cracker, shedding the duvet and the stapler. Mrs Prince steps back with a gasp. She takes a deep breath, relaxes her shoulders, and smiles at me. I'm impressed. She must have done intervention training.

"Oh, July, I startled you awake. Sorry. I didn't mean to. Why are you sitting there, child? You should be on the bed." She picks up the stapler. "I wondered where this was. Good news, Mr McNeil says because it's Friday you can leave early. Here is your Permission Slip. Now go straight home." She spreads the duvet neatly on the bed and switches off the heater. "Don't come back until you're well. We don't need the flu spreading to the whole school."

I leave, making sure that no one is waiting for me on the stairs or along the corridor. Exiting the school through the private staff entrance, I sprint down the footpath through the school's forest, planted a hundred years ago by the school founders for privacy, to the bus stop. Nobody stands in my way. The bus arrives as I get there.

On the bus, I realize that I'm out of dagga for Mom. She needs it. Watching her in pain breaks my heart and I'll do anything to make both our pains stop. With Richter out to kill me, I need a new dealer. Maybe Kevin will sell me a couple of joints. He'll be rigging at Mark's party tonight along with Richter. Good sense says I avoid the place, but I don't have a choice. Mom needs it.

3. AT MARK'S PARTY

MARK LIVES IN WATERKLOOF. I jump off the bus expecting to see mansions, but each home hides behind its own massive wall topped with a metal tiara of clicking electricity. All have fully automated, and closed, entrance gates. I hurry up the hill.

The gates to Mark's place are open. No one here leaves their gates open. They even hire security guards to open and close gates if there is a party. Why buy a safe then leave the door open?

My brain swirls down a worm hole: have the bad people invaded this school party? If they have, I don't know what they look like, how they act, who they hang out with. What if they join with Richter? I'm one against possibly hundreds. I can't die now. Who will take care of Mom? She'll be alone. She'll die.

"My! What a pretty belly button," I recall Mom say and I chuckle. She's right. I need to change my focus. I'm not the only thing on Richter's mind. I feel my head pop out of the fear bubble. Yes there's still a price on me, but I knew this when I chose to come here. Mom deserves to be comfortable. She needs Mary Jane and I'll get it for her because I love her. Open gates or not, my mission hasn't changed—I must find Kevin, buy the dagga, and leave without alerting Richter to my presence.

That doesn't mean I'm stupid enough to walk into a trap.

Cautiously I step forward and scope out the area. Four

floodlights illuminate the silky lawns and the curving, tree-lined avenue all the way down to the circular driveway and the massive front door. Creeping from tree shadow to tree shadow I get as close as possible to the house and hide behind an old jacaranda tree. Next task: find Kevin.

A wide terrace flanks the front door. It's occupied by some of the school's smokers, puffing away, creating clouds, imagining they look grown-up and sophisticated.

Kevin is a chain smoker, therefore predictable. He can't go fifteen minutes without a smoke and so will definitely come outside. It's a starting point. I'll wait the quarter hour and see. Within five minutes he appears from the side of the house. He walks up the driveway, leans back against a car, and lights up a smoke. He's dressed in jeans and a dark green bomber jacket.

Staying in the shadows I move in on him. He might shop me to Richter the second he sees me, but I'm prepared. My new flick knife is in my pocket; its handle warms my hand. If anyone attacks me, I intend to leave them with identifying wounds, nothing that clothing can hide. I will aim for the head and face, marking them as predators.

I reach the tree closest to him and call, "Hey Kevin, I need six joints for my mom. I can't ask anyone else." He jumps, but doesn't look at me. I take that as a good sign.

After a slow drag on his smoke he says, "Stupid move! Richter's here, right here." He pushes off from the car and heads towards the house.

I didn't risk my life to be brushed aside like ash off his sleeve. I break cover and run after him. "No! Wait! Please! My mom's super sick. She needs it so badly. You have the stuff. I have cash. Please help me!" He sidesteps me and keeps walking.

"Get out now while you can! Stupid! Just so you know, you're not invisible in that black hoodie." He sounds scared. Flicking away the cigarette butt, he runs up the curved front stairs and into the house.

Retracing my steps through the trees, I hear the sound of something heavy falling to the ground. Scrabbling like a rabbit under the nearest bush, I freeze, ears, nose, and eyes fully on alert. Are they here, waiting for me? The sound was very close.

Suddenly I'm encased in total darkness. My brain screams, "HOOD!" and I reach up to rip it off, but I touch air and my face. Am I blind? No, I'm not. All four of the big overhead security lights have died. That's weird; all four, simultaneously. I heard on the news that home invasions happen a lot in large homes. That explains the open gates. I got that right. I must leave. Whatever fell nearby, it means I'm too close to the action. The criminals are working right here.

It's so black no one can see me, but if I move they'll hear me. Kevin's words flash into my mind. He tried to warn me, which means this is all planned: a scheme of Richter's.

The thought reignites my urgent need to escape. I don't want to be caught in his dragnet. I get up, barely take five steps before I trip and fall. The object that tripped me is warm, solid, and definitely human.

The human mumbles.

Female human.

Adrenalin pumps through my body. I heave the girl up and drag her under a clump of thick bushes. My heart is juddering like an engine. Stroking the hoodie off her face, I recognize Andie Elliot. She's in all my classes. Then I see the cigarette burns on her neck. Time stops. She is me one week ago. I tremble in terror.

She mumbles, "Luke, Luke, Luke . . . "

I don't need to, but I unzip her hoodie and find bleeding arcs tracking down her neck, the same arcs that mark my own body. I know definitively that the man who raped me has raped Andie.

He is here. Close by.

I hug her tightly and drag us even further under the bushes as an ice wall of dread collapses over me. My eyes flicker, my ears buzz, my knees rattle against each other. My guts coil and cramp. I think I will vomit or shit or both. I can't breathe. Helpless, I let the tsunami sweep me away.

The scent of dirt, pine and leaves greets me when I come to. My back aches from lying on a root. My right arm is numb from holding Andie. She is silent. The date rape drug they gave her has kicked in.

A loud mechanical whir starts.

Behind me, through the trees, I can see the home's large garage with its three bays. The middle door opens. Standing there are Andre Vermarck, Mpho Kageso, and Leyton Donaldson, the grade 12 boys who handed me to the rapist, all core members of the Richter Gang. They're in black hoodies, black jeans, and black boots.

I pull Andie even further under the bushes and hug her tight.

Footsteps walk the tarmac. I hear bushes rustling. The boys move closer to us. Feet appear next to us. I can see the bad stitching on the hem of someone's jeans.

"The goods should be here ready for pick-up, right here under these trees, those were the instructions," Leyton says. "Something's gone wrong. Let's split. Fast. We'll go collect the first parcel."

Their steps fade, the garage door hums shut, darkness settles. I'm grateful for its heavy veil.

I rock Andie like a baby and whisper, "I've got you. You're safe now. You're alive." But I don't know what to do next. I can't get the two of us out of here safely. I came on a bus. We need someone with a car. I can't go looking for a ride, not with

Leyton and his friends here.

Someone is stumbling through the bushes. Did one of the boys stay behind to try and flush Andie out? They're getting closer.

Unable to move, I slip off my big jacket and put it backwards on Andie, tying the cords to hide her face. No one needs to see her like this. People judge raped girls, making out they deserved it, calling them a tease and a whore. I can protect Andie. I push her behind me.

David McNeil crashes down on top of me. I take an elbow in the ribs and a knee in the stomach. Winded, I kick at him and keep kicking until he rolls away.

He says, "Shit! I'm sorry. Did I hurt you? It all went dark. I was over by the . . . oh . . . it's you, July." His tone changes, hardens, as if I don't deserve any apology. "What's that?" He spots Andie and moves closer. I don't trust him at all. Why is he here? I don't believe in coincidence.

I stand up and block his way. "Hey, scoot. Go puke somewhere else."

He bristles. "I'm not drunk. I needed fresh air. Is that a body?" He edges forward all thrilled curiosity.

"So? Go suck it some place else." I'm close enough to smell the beer on his breath. He might be tall but I will not let him see Andie. He retreats one step then crouches down and tries to touch Andie around me. I plant my boot a millimetre away from his fingers. We lock eyes. He retracts his hand and stands up like an agitated bull preparing to charge. I fold my arms and wait. His jeans are covered in dirt as is his t-shirt. What was he doing before he fell on us?

"What happened here?" he asks as if he has the right to know.

"None of your business. Go away." I don't trust this good-looking second son of the principal. He thinks he farts *eau de cologne* because he can kick a rugby ball between the uprights.

"Just tell me it's alive."

"Yes. Go away."

"Who is it?"

"No one you know."

"Try me. I know everyone." He widens his stance as if preparing for a tackle on the rugby field. I put my right hand in my pocket and hold my knife. If he touches me I will hurt him.

"We need to get home," I say. He relaxes.

"I can carry him to the house," he says. "You can't, you're tiny."

I do need help. "Fine, but no blabbing about this to anyone, okay? The car is waiting at the gazebo." Why did I say that? There's no way I can find an open car to turn my lie into reality. This is South Africa: an unlocked car is a stolen car.

He lifts Andie up fireman-style, draping her over his shoulder then flashes me a grin. "So a girl then; bumps in all the right places. Why is her coat on backwards?"

"Leave it that way. No one needs to know who she is."

"She needs help. Are you helping her?" He really does sound concerned. Is it guilt?

"We both are right now."

"You mean I'm now guilty by association. Harsh. As long as you do what you say and keep her safe I'll play it your way. Is it a secret? Do we pretend this never happened?"

"How much do you want your father to know about this evening?" I ask, nailing him in his soft spot. He's terrified of his father. Rumour has it Mr McNeil canes his sons.

David turns to glare at me. "Fine. This never happened."

At the gazebo a Mazda 323 is idling. I notice its back door

not quite closed.

Recognizing another gift from the universe, I say, "There's the car. Put her on the back seat."

He does, then stands up and flicks his long fringe out of his eyes. "Don't mention me and I won't mention you." He walks back to the house.

I gently remove my coat from Andie. On a scrap of paper I write down her name and what I can recall of her address then tuck it into her jeans pocket.

Hearing voices, I see a man and woman approaching the vehicle. I gently close the backdoor and step behind the gazebo. As they drive off I record the car registration number.

It's the best I can do. Andie is away from here. I must run to catch the 10:30 bus. Leyton's words ring in my ears. They are collecting a first parcel. That could be me. They know where I live. Tonight I will sleep at the school.

4. BLACK FEATHERS

FINGERS SHAKING WITH FEAR, I open the padlock to the pedestrian gate at the west entrance to the school. Above me, the school has dissolved into the dark mass of the steep hill. My breath comes out white in the cold. Are Richter's dogs waiting for me? They'll be in cars. My heart beats like a warning drum, urging me to hurry. I duck into the forest and start climbing, keeping the beam of my flashlight on my feet. It's a hard slog, but I take the school without a battle.

The sickroom has its own bathroom. I shower and climb into bed, my knife under my pillow. Staring at the ceiling, black featherlike strands cover my vision, leaving me blind. I panic, pat the bed. I'm not dreaming. I can feel the sheet, the duvet, and the pillow. Helpless, I curl up into a ball around the pillow, blinking to clear my eyes. I fail.

The stench of cigarette smoke, sour beer, and fresh blood is all around me, suffocating me. I'm back in last Friday night. A vice holds my head and I can't look away. The rapist arrives. My scream stops in my mouth. I push myself against the wall but don't actually move. My body doesn't belong to me.

The rapist stands still, hands in his pockets.

I can't look away. My vision zooms in. Specimen: rapist. A dark blue mask covers his lower face. He is white, has a tan. Forehead smooth. Hair blond, crew cut. Round eye sockets, eyes blue, sky not sea, eyebrows straight and apart, a haughty tilt to the head. He wears grey dress pants, polished black shoes, a white shirt, sleeves neatly folded to expose his wrists.

Do I recognize him? No. I don't know him. Is he a schoolboy? No. Older, probably in his mid or late twenties.

The picture fades. My vision clears. I pull the duvet up over my head and lie still. Am I going insane? Maybe finding Andie tonight pushed me over the edge. Any stability I gained in the past week is gone. My mind is bleeding with my body. How do you heal a mind? You can't clean it with Dettol and take Panado for the pain. Is my vision a message pointing me to a cure? Will revealing the rapist heal me? Reveal to whom?

I brain-tumble out of my safe-warm bed into last Friday's Brooklyn Police Station. It's a two-room bungalow that smells of pee and vomit, seasoned with dirty mop and bleach. It makes me want to puke. Speckles decorate the walls: yellow, green, and brown: pee, snot, and shit?

Behind the high wooden counter, three white policemen neatly dressed in blue uniforms watch me limp towards them. They don't offer me a chair or invite me into the private office at the back. They leer down at me, waiting for me to speak.

The twenty-six letters of the alphabet circle around my head but refuse to arrange themselves into words that describe my ordeal. Deprived of their help, I stand silent, my clothes torn, my body bruised and burned, my blood dripping on the floor. I am fifteen and three days old. Why that figure stuck in my head I don't know. Maybe I thought they'd ask my age.

The short policeman says, "Speak up. We don't have all night. Come on."

I walked for an hour in the dark to get here.

Can they not see my condition? Why don't they help me? Isn't that their job? Mom said if I ever needed serious help, I must call the police, not the security company we pay to look after the flat.

Impatient, the short one says, "Hey! Listen up. You know what happens to women who walk the streets at night. What do you expect? Good girls stay home."

"Look here." The fat policeman stabs a pudgy finger at a poster on the wall, "Read: 'Every thirty seconds somewhere in South Africa a woman is raped'. How do you think we *made* that statistic? Now you know. Live and learn."

The words lash at my violated body. Live and learn. Mom was wrong.

Any remnants of my faith in the police crumble. Here again, this same evening, I witness men with no compassion at all. They don't see a child, a human, they see a female body they can use and throw away. What makes them blind?

The tall policeman says, "If you want a lift home, call a taxi. There's a pay phone outside." He shakes his head and turns to his colleagues, "Stupid kid. Thinks we give a shit about rape. On our petrol rations! If it isn't mass murder, we won't come. I thought the public knew that."

Now I know why men rape; because no one stops them.

My alarm clock reads 2:00 am. What was it about Andie's rape that started me mind-tripping? I pause and repeat the two words *Andie's rape* until I hear the deeper question, the one bothering me: Why did he choose her?

Andromeda Elliot and I have very little in common. We both attend Blue Ridge College. We're both in grade ten. We're both girls. We are both girls. Nothing else on the list puts you under threat of rape.

I feel like I've stepped out of jail into bright sunlight. After my rape, I blamed myself. Because I bought dagga from Richter I put myself in danger. Now I know that is not true. The rapist violated me because he could. My actions didn't come into it. And why Andie was at the party doesn't matter either. He broke the law because the police do not take this law seriously and he knows no-one will punish him. He is a criminal. Hurting women is wrong even if the law and the police don't stop it.

If no one stops him he will do it again.

I know what he looks like. I know if I follow Richter he'll lead me to the rapist. I can try to stop him. No! I can't stop him. Why would I do such a thing? My aim is to stay as far away from him and his thugs as possible. I want to live. That's why I'm in this bed at school and not at home.

Like a mosquito, the idea keeps buzzing in my head. I think about what it will take to take down the rapist. I must evade his gate-keepers, boys like Richter and his gang. He probably has lots of schoolboy gangs selling his muck. I have no car, no friends, no fortified castle, and no AK-47 machine guns. It's a stupid idea.

Andie's father is a very wealthy man. The police will investigate her assault. It's their job.

Who am I kidding? They won't, but they will pretend to be doing something. They like those rape statistics.

He'll do it again if no one stops him. Buzz. Buzz.

I wish I could do something. But I am one, alone, with my little spitting knife, hiding under a duvet in the school sickroom.

What else do I know about the rapist? He goes to Blue Ridge parties. He rapes Blue Ridge girls. Did he go to Blue Ridge? Is that how Richter met him?

My head aches. If I don't sleep I'll be even more of a basket case in the morning.

Mom and I used to pray together at night. I would sleep well back then. I'm ready to try anything. I whisper, "Please let Andie get home safely. Let me not have screwed that up. And please take away Mom's pain. Thanks."

I set my alarm for 6:00 am. I will spend the whole day with Mom. Counting all the locked gates and doors between me and any intruder, I finally fall asleep.

5. HIPPOPOTAMUS

"GOOD MORNING, JULY," Mrs Gresham says as I enter the hospice. For a short, plump woman she moves gracefully on her low-heeled, white shoes. A white, leather belt cinches in the waist of her soft pink dress, and a pink band restrains her chin-length, greying, blonde hair.

"Come into my office. I need to borrow a little of your time."

A surge of fear leaves me dizzy. I've never been in her inner sanctum. We usually share quick greetings through her sliding window.

She takes my arm and guides me in to a pink leather sofa. I look at her fingers. She doesn't have a wedding ring. Mom doesn't have one either.

"July, today you need to be extra courageous." She takes my hand.

Dust motes spin in the shaft of light streaming in through the window.

"Your mom has pneumonia and isn't responding to treatment. The doctor arrived early this morning. Fluid is flooding her lungs. She's struggling to breathe. Her poor little body has no fight left. She's very fragile . . . "

I hear the loud ticking of the wall clock. "Please may I go and see her now?"

"Yes. Go. I'll be close by." Mrs Gresham releases my hand.

The foyer leads out into a paved, central square with a high thatched roof. On all the sides are the in-patient rooms, each with a yellow door. Each door displays a carving of an African animal but no room number.

My mom's room is marked with a hippopotamus.

"Hi Mommy. I'm here," I say, too shaken to fake cheerfulness.

"Love . . . come," Mom says, her voice thin, breathless, cracked.

Moving around the metal IV stand with its three fat plastic bags of liquid uselessness, I notice mom's dull yellow pee in the bag hanging under the bed.

A steamer bubbles in a corner, Mom loves the sound. A simple A4-size wooden cross hangs on the wall where she can see it. Thirty-six vanilla-scented candles of different shapes and sizes line up on the window ledge, one for each year of Mom's life. She said their twinkling lights and smell will remind her of birthday cakes and happier times. A tremor runs through me. I recognize each item from her Final Day list. Dread feels heavier than fear. It sinks into your chest and presses on your heart, crushing down to your core to plant its seeds of pain for an everlasting harvest.

Sitting on the high, narrow bed, I rest my hand gently on her leg, scared of hurting her. The silver blankets and white sheets come from her own bedroom. In a frame on the bedside table stands a laughing three-year-old me on my first bike. Mom's all-time favourite memory. She said it shows my inborn love of life and determination.

She reaches out her right arm, purple from all the morphine injections, and searches for my hand. When she finds it, she holds it tight.

"Love . . . you." Each word forced out with effort.

I climb on the bed and curl up against her, my face against her beating chest. Here is my comfort and my strength, the only person who cares for me. Here I can be a child. Mom will carry the weight of the world for me.

I feel her every bone. This skeleton contains my precious

mother: twinkling blue eyes of laughter in the morning and funky dancing at night. An emergency-room nurse who believed all people deserve respect, who contracted HIV when an angry patient plunged a needle into her leg.

Mom strokes my hair. "Love you. Always. My heart. My baby."

I lean over and kiss her on her damp forehead. "Love you too, Mommy. Always and forever. What can I do?"

"Take paper." She opens her left fist. It holds a yellow Post-it note.

I sit up and take it. It says,

Julius Stedman

082 808 5666

Mom says, "He's your father. Knows."

I stare at the words, dazed. Why would Mom invite an unknown man into this room now? Has she sent for him? Will he walk in and claim me like lost baggage? I don't want him.

Mom fumbles for my hand. "He will. I can't."

What kind of selfish jerk am I? I push the note into my pocket and focus on Mom. She needs me now. I can feel sorry for myself later. I lie back down and snuggle up against her.

"Thank you, Mommy. You always care about me. I love that. I'll hang on to it, just in case, you know, like you say 'you need to be prepared for life', hey. You don't have to worry about me. I'm doing fine."

"Your hair?"

"I know. Pretty bad, hey? I did it myself. Hairdressers are expensive. I'll get better with practice."

"Yes." She always believed in saving.

"And, Mom, I will become an accountant, like you want, okay? That way I'll learn how to make money work for me. I'm already ahead of the others in my class—I've got the flat."

"Paid off." It's her biggest success, leaving me a fully paid-off home and some money in the bank. I don't have to fall into the hands of Child Welfare.

"What do you think of my new coat?"

"Too big."

"Oh, that's the style now. It has tons of pockets, and it's so warm. Feel the wool on the inside." I take her hand to place it on my coat. It feels very heavy.

"Mom?" The ribcage under my cheek fails to rise.

"Mommy? Mom!"

Mrs Gresham enters the room.

I sit up, not letting go of Mom's hand. It couldn't be. No life glistens in those beloved blue eyes. The distance between there and here can't be one missed breath. Two seconds ago she voiced an opinion. How could death be so close, so quick?

Mrs Gresham brushes closed Mom's eyes.

"I've called the doctor, Sweetie. You sit here as long as you need. I'll be right outside the door." She places a blanket on my lap, pats my shoulder, and leaves the room, closing the door.

God, if you are there what do I do now? No answer arrives. I'm alone.

I lie down next to Mom and take her hand. Silence covers us. Mom insisted that at death people move into a place of all knowledge. I stroke her hand and whisper,

"You are right, Mom, the coat is too big. I bought it for all its pockets inside and out. They come in handy. See, my knife fits in perfectly. Yes. I am in danger. A boy called Travis Richter wants to kill me. By now you know that last Friday when I collected your dagga, I was raped. I escaped. Now they want me dead. Last night I slept in my school's sick room. It's safer than our flat. He raped Andie last night. If you know the rapist's name could you give it to me? I have to stop him hurting any more girls. No girl should feel like this. I wanted to ask you about my eyesight; it's playing tricks on me. You'd know the answer." I lean on my elbow and study Mom's face, brush my fingers across her cheek, and feel the skin drawn tight over the bones. "I need you, Mom. You are my anchor. You hold me together. I love you so much."

Cool air drifts along my arm, lingers on my cheek then rises and touches my nose. I recognize our bedtime ritual and kiss her on the forehead.

"Night, Mommy." I get up and leave the room.

Outside, under the thatched roof in the lapa, I find a chair and sit down. I feel shapeless as though an eraser has rubbed away the borders of my body.

I watch the doctor and Mrs Gresham enter Mom's room. The undertakers arrive, emerging shortly after with a narrow stretcher and a zipped body bag. Death has done its worst. I marvel at how quickly humans erase all trace of its crime.

6. AFTER DEATH

I SIT ON THE PINK leather sofa next to Mrs Gresham listening to her. There's a cup of tea on the wooden coffee table. I think it's mine. My hands, jaw, kneecaps, and ankles tremble like aspen leaves in a summer storm. I am aware of the world all around me, but I am not in it.

Mrs Gresham takes my hand. I can't hear her, but her words hang in the air like instructional banners on After Death choices. I read:

- Run away and pretend nothing happened.
- Lose yourself in grief and forget to live your own life.
- Accept the permanence of the change and live your new reality.

I see a pine coffin lying on a freshly mowed lawn. A woman in a flowing dress approaches the box. She tears it in half, kicks in the sides, jumps up and down on it, pulverizing the wood until it forms two shining painted Dutch clogs. Satisfied with her creation, she slips them on and walks away. I nod in admiration. I want to mould my life to suit myself. My first job now is to make sure I am safe.

My mother is dead.

Mrs Gresham is still talking.

There's a black door slowly opening behind her. I'm surprised Mrs Gresham doesn't shiver in the cold draft. I do, gooseflesh spreads over my body. They say it means someone has walked over your grave, which proves I have a grave. I will die. That is comforting. I'll see Mom again. Why is the door black? I don't want to know. Death in western culture is coloured black. I read somewhere that the colour of death in China is white. Why does the end of life need a colour? It should be a nothing colour—clear, transparent, empty.

Mrs Gresham initiates me into a new club: Girls with Dead Mothers. It's my second involuntary club sign-up—last Friday I joined the Raped Girls Club. They are both secret clubs—no fees and no parties, and they don't advertise for membership, others do all the recruiting.

Mrs Gresham speaks death lingo. "Your mom planned the whole service. You'll see a plain pine coffin. The preacher has the scriptures, music, and handouts. I did not publish her passing in any paper. She was firm on this. It must be kept private."

I can hear Mom saying, "Keep it quiet for one year. We don't want Child Welfare coming to investigate and deciding you belong in an orphanage. Next year, when you turn sixteen they can't touch you. I don't want you in the hands of those people."

Over the months I absorbed Mom's distrust of the people who work with teenage girls in the state system. She never told me what started her fear, but I trust her information. No one must know that I am an orphan.

Except that Julius Stedman exists. The paper in my pocket is a passage to a new world. Why did Mom keep him from me? What is wrong with him? Why didn't they marry? He sounds shifty.

"The funeral is at 3:00 pm at the Sunnyside Baptist Church. You can wear black if you like. Close family usually do. The Ladies' Auxiliary will cater the reception. Don't expect a black hatchback hearse; nowadays it's usually a silver minivan."

I feel sick. I want to go home. Mom will make me hot sweet tea and Marmite toast, take my temperature, and tuck me into bed with a hot water bottle, an arm tickle, and a nose kiss.

"Please may I go?" I ask, surprised that my voice still operates.

Mrs Gresham nods. "I would like it if you came and stayed with me for a couple of days at least. I'd enjoy looking after you."

I get up and walk to the door. "I'll think about it."

"I'll phone you to see how you are. Keep your phone on." She walks with me to the front door, gives me a hug. She's warm and smells of lavender.

"Yes. I will." I mean it. She's my direct link to Mom. She knew her. We can share our knowledge and keep Mom alive that way.

"And go straight home."

The thing is I don't know where home is right now. I leave the hospice, turn right and head for Magnolia Dell. Two hours later, I find myself at school sitting on the grandstand watching boys play rugby. The under-sixteens are losing to Lyttelton Manor High School. I can see the problem. David McNeil isn't playing.

Walking down the driveway with the after-game crowd, I exit the main gate and catch a bus home. Dropping my keys in the red vase on the table by the door, I head straight into the kitchen and switch on the kettle and the radio. 702 blares out the Mango Groove hit "Special Star." I imagine Mom dancing while peeling potatoes. She liked potatoes but she said she didn't have any Irish in her, only Anglo-Saxon. I teased her that the British aren't known for their natural rhythm. She warned me to watch out as I'm a 50-50 blend. We laughed a lot together. I never asked her about the other fifty percent. I didn't want to know.

Mom, you know I'm thinking about finding the man who

raped me. I don't want him hurting any other girl, or killing me. He said he would. I have his note. He raped Andie. You said the police would help me, but they blamed me instead. They mocked me. No one wants to stop this rapist. It's unfair. If a fox gets into a chicken coop, you kill the fox and build a stronger coop, but a man destroys the life of a woman and everyone looks the other way? Something is very wrong. I'm not brave, Mom, but I don't want any girl feeling like this, like we are not human, not valuable, just disposable trash like a soiled hamburger wrapper.

I want to do something, but what? Try to get rid of the rapist. How?

The copper lamp shines and the carpet sparkles. The kettle clicks off; water boiled. Mom doesn't answer. Any decision I make is mine alone as are the consequences.

Checking the security gate and the front door, I climb into my own bed and pull the soft blankets up over my head. I know nothing will be better tomorrow, but at least it won't be today, the day my mother died.

7. MONDAY

I'M SITTING HERE ON A ROCK in the middle of the school's forest, which occupies part of the grounds. I got off the bus and began up the driveway until the tears arrived. Not delicate little drops you can sniff back, but a harsh, deep-gulping, can't-breathe, throat-rupturing flood. I had to hide. My nose is dripping snot like Victoria Falls. With no tissues left and no sign of this stopping, I'll have to go home. If the teachers see me like this they'll ask questions I can't answer.

A twig snaps and a few birds flap away into the air. Someone is approaching. Two steps crackle gingerly on the dead leaves. Richter still wants me dead.

I run, not on the cleared path but straight up the slope. I need to lose him, but he's moving fast, stomping on shrubs and pushing through bushes, birds screeching angrily above him.

"July! July Abraham! I know it's you. Stop! I want to talk to you."

David McNeil! He sounds furious as he scrambles up the slope like a baboon.

"Hey! July! Stop! Just answer one question. Hey! Wait up! I'm faster than you. I will catch you." His long strides close the space between us. One flying rugby tackle and he'll grab me. I know he will.

My knees tremble, the climb is steep. I can't escape him. I feel in my pocket for my knife.

He arrives, face scratched, blazer torn, leaves in his hair, and shoes covered in dust. He sees me and stops dead two metres away, panting.

"I helped you," he says, attempting to speak quietly. "Now help me. Who was the girl we put into the Mazda?" His fists are clenched at his sides. "Andie Elliot is missing. Did you know that? Andie Elliott. She didn't get home. Who did we put in that car? Tell me!"

Guilt drops on me. My legs buckle under this added burden. I sit down on the ground and hug my knees. I didn't help Andie. I made it worse. I'm an idiot. Why did I ever get involved?

David sits down to face me. He hands me a large white tissue. I didn't even realize I was crying. He waits at least a minute before speaking.

"Was that Andie? Her father phoned my dad, he thinks she was with me all night. My dad's grounded me until I tell what I know. I'm not allowed to play rugby. I missed Saturday's game. We lost."

"Were you at the party with her?" I ask, wiping my face.

"We danced. She came with Khetiwe. The girls hung out upstairs mostly with Gigi, Mark's sister." He flicks his fringe out of his eyes. He has black hair, way too long by school standards. I'm surprised his father lets him get away with it. I blow my nose. The tears stop.

"So you were with her." I still doubt his absolute innocence.

He bristles. "We danced together. We are not an item. She came with Khetiwe."

"Why is that important?"

He clenches his jaw and breathes heavily through his nose. "Because I am responsible for a girlfriend's safety, I know that. My dad has said it enough times in the last twenty-four hours that it's tattooed on my brain, but she isn't my girlfriend. She arrived with Khetiwe. Which means Khetiwe and her had a plan to get home. I didn't know their plan. Why would I?"

"What did Khetiwe say?"

"She said Andie was with me. That's a lie! She started all this!" He struggles to speak calmly. He stands up, paces a couple of laps around a tree. "If I can just tell them we put Andie in the car, they will know she isn't missing."

But I know what I did. I know Andie really is missing. I can't help him. I don't want any attention falling on me. Not now. My mother is dead. I am alone. I have to protect myself.

He comes back to me and sits down. "So was it Andie we put in the Mazda that came to fetch her?" He looks me in the eye, searching for the truth.

"It was Andie. It wasn't her car."

He stares at me and I watch as my words move down his pinball alley brain, sparking and pinging each time they hit an obstacle.

"She was sick . . . we left her in a stranger's car . . . how nuts are you, July?" Now he's really mad at me. "You should have told me! We had her safe. Why the hell would you stuff her into a stranger's car? You're crazy!" He stands up, shoulders his bag. "I'm going to tell my dad. This is serious. You're in such trouble!"

"No, you are," I say, keeping my voice low.

He glares at me, steps closer, as if to threaten me.

"Oh no! No way! None of this was my idea. I helped you. This is all you." But he doesn't walk off. He's unsure of himself. Good!

My own survival depends on shutting this boy up good and tight. If Richter knows I helped Andie escape he'll hunt me with even more hate. I stand up, shoulder my bag, and pat the knife in my pocket to reassure myself. I start heading for the main driveway with its crowds of arriving students. He follows like I expect.

"This is what I know," I whisper. He speeds up and walks beside me. "Andie is dumped outside. You come along asking to help move her away; a coincidence, perhaps. You have all your rugby friends inside the house. You know Gigi and the girls are upstairs. You know we are moving a girl. You say nothing at all. You just let it happen. Why? That's the bigger question here. If they ask me, that's what I will say."

I hear him hiss in disgust. "You don't care, do you? Andie is missing and you don't care to help her." He speeds up and leaves me behind.

He is so very wrong. I do care. I helped because I cared. I knew exactly what had happened to Andie. He doesn't know what it is to be raped.

A tremor shudders through me. Until my own rape, I hadn't known. It's kept a secret, but it doesn't protect the girls, it protects the boys.

I have to shut David up. My life depends on it. I can't have police and Child Welfare digging into my affairs. Not now. I slow down and stay close to a group of chatty grade eights.

David is failing in Afrikaans, algebra, and accounting. Does his father know? If I fill out three Intervention Request slips and put them in Mr McNeil's hands, I might toss David down a deep well of trouble. Then he'll have to leave me alone.

I'll get the Intervention Request slips from the office.

8. RUMOURS

AFTER LEAVING THE INTERVENTION Request slips on Mrs Prince's desk, I sit down on a bench in the east quad across from the staffroom windows. No one can hurt me here. Prefects walk past on their way to the prefects' room, assuming some staff member has ordered me here as punishment. The bell will ring in five minutes.

David's older brother, Peter, a prefect, strolls down the cloister with Leigh-Anne du Toit, another grade twelve, clamped to his arm: two blondes aware of their own beauty. Although Peter has an official girlfriend, Colleen Jenkins, also blonde, he never discourages the girls who flock around him. In a Disney Movie version of Blue Ridge College, Peter would be the Prince. When the McNeil brothers enter a room, nobody notices David. I distrust Peter. He sees girls as decorations, not people.

In registration class the rumour mill is hot with details about Andie Elliot's disappearance. She ended up in Mamelodi, or Danville; she's raped, has HIV; her hair has been shaved off, her hands chopped off; she's dead, she was necklaced. I can imagine the necklacing: a car tire filled with petrol hung about her slender neck, matches lit and tossed into the tire, the wall of flames and black smoke rising up. I want to say none of it could be true, but I know my country, and all of it can be true. How could I be stupid enough to put her in that Mazda? If she's dead I am a murderer.

During geography, I hear the purr of a mobile phone and watch Khetiwe put her hand into her blazer pocket. The noise stops. A note then travels to Lily. Both are Andie's closest friends.

Mrs Horack hones in on me.

"Pay attention, July, face the board, please. Can you give me one characteristic of a subduction zone?"

She points with her pen to the diagram on the screen. If she heard the mobile phone, she's decided not to mention it, expecting Khetiwe to behave responsibly.

I read a label on the diagram. "New islands are created by the volcanoes." It proves satisfactory and I'm saved. But I've missed Lily's expression as she read the note.

Five minutes before first break, the classroom intercom springs to life.

"David McNeil, David McNeil to Mr McNeil's office. David McNeil to the headmaster's office immediately."

Everyone, even Sesi Mopeli, who never raises her doe eyes above foot level, swivels in their seats to gawk at David, relishing the instant thrill of witnessing the father-son relationship morph into that of principal-student.

Chris Harrods, David's best friend, prods David between the shoulder blades. "Hey, dorf brain. Climb off planet Honey and get to your dad's office pronto."

Irritated, David pulls away. "Don't rush me. I'm getting there." But he doesn't move.

"Quickly please, David," Mrs Horack says. "I have a lesson to finish."

"Yes, Ma'am, I just . . . um . . . well . . . I'm not sure why . . . "

Mark says, "It's tough being brain dead." The class laughs.

Leaning forward, David smacks Mark's head into the classroom wall. Mark jumps up fists lifted. The class takes a collective breath in happy anticipation.

"Stop it! Enough!" Mrs Horack shouts. "David, please leave."

"Yes, Ma'am." David packs his books into his bag, fastens the buckles and heads for the door like a condemned man approaching the scaffold.

"Some admin mistake," Johnny offers as solace. I know he's wrong. David is about to walk into the minefield that was my doing.

The bell rings. Mrs Horack sighs and puts her book on her desk.

"Pack up class. You may go."

Khetiwe and Lily hurry out. I follow them, ever vigilant for any of Richter's dogs.

The two girls head straight to the Media Centre, pushing their way through to the very back of the long central reading room. They settle down at a table hidden behind a high shelf of encyclopedias. I stand on the other side as close to them as possible.

Khetiwe says, "Andie's at home, but her dad won't let her see anyone. She sounded shaky."

My stomach unclenches and I lean against the shelf in relief. I'm not a murderer.

"What actually happened to her?" Lily asks.

"No details."

"But she's alive," Lily says. "That's a good thing."

"Why do we say that? What if being alive sucks? She sounded zombie-like. She said at the hospital they brought in a psychologist and a policewoman."

"Which means it's something really bad, at the very least, rape," Lily says.

"They are moving away from Gauteng as soon as possible."

"That bad. And it all started at Mark's party. You were there, did you see a stranger?"

"No. I saw David and Andie locked together all night."

"David? You think he raped her?" Lily sounds shocked. "I don't believe you."

"She only went there to see him. I went because she wanted to be there to see him. They spent the whole time together, so who else but David?" Khetiwe says angrily.

"Whoever it is, it means there's a rapist among us, right now. Here," Lily says.

They go silent. I know the rapist isn't a schoolboy, but I can't tell them and expose myself as an eavesdropper.

"How do we know if we're next?" Lily asks. "How do we not be next?"

"We don't go to any more parties," Khetiwe says. "I'm going to carry my mace with me all the time."

"I'm phoning my mom to collect me after school," Lily says. "I don't want to take the bus. Do you want a lift?"

"Yes! I do! Come with me, I have to go to the toilet. I think we should stay together at all times."

Lily says, "The safest quad is east quad. No one will hurt us there."

I watch the girls leave, and then move to a desk where the librarian can see me. Warmth infuses me, running up and down from my heart. It feels like my whole body is thrilled. By putting Andie in that car I got her home safely. I did something right. My small intervention changed events and saved Andie's life. I have power. Maybe I can help Lily and Khetiwe and all the Blue Ridge girls stay safe by finding the rapist. With my mom dead, no one needs me anymore. I have nothing to lose.

9. CONTACT

CAUGHT! A CORNER OF A SHARP cement step cuts into my left shoulder blade as Leyton Donaldson pushes me against the stairs near the girls' change rooms. His hand wraps around my throat, pushing heavily against my windpipe. I can't scream, I can hardly breathe as he leans on me, forcing my face into his armpit.

"Richter says to kill you," he snarls.

His breath smells like shit. Did he eat it for breakfast? Talk about a dangerous weapon. Where is everyone? Will he really kill me here? Stars flicker before my eyes, as I start to choke. He laughs and leans in even harder. There is no one to help me.

With my numbed brain, I remember my knife. My right hand is free. I inch my knife out from my pocket. I've never done this before. I'll get this one chance. I have to do it now. But I falter. I can't do this. I have to. I want to live. No one is coming to help.

Slowly I twist, lift my hand behind his back, find his belt, guess where his kidneys are, release the blade. What I didn't consider was all the warm blood spurting over my hand, along my arm, dripping on the ground at our feet; marking me.

He makes a feral, high pitched scream and pushes me away. "What the hell, you bitch . . . " He crumples silently to the ground. I gulp air into my starved lungs.

If I run through the school looking like bloody Lady Macbeth someone will notice. It's too far to go to the girls' toilets in the south quad. I'm supposed to be in maths with Mr van Zyl. I slip into the staff toilet nearby and bolt the door. My white school shirt is red from cuff to elbow, my blue blazer has a soaked brown flash down the sleeve and the front pocket.

Stripping down, I clean myself and my clothes. My throat aches. I look in the mirror. My neck is bruised red. My eyes are so large I look like an owl. My hair is its usual chaotic spikes.

I start to shake. I did it. I'm alive. I protected myself. First steps are hard. Now, no one will ever consider me a soft target, but they will take it as a declaration of war.

The dark blue of the blazer hides its wetness, but I smell like a wet dog. I clean my knife and drop it back in my pocket. It is exactly the right weapon for me; quiet and deadly, together we won our first battle. Checking that the basin is clean, I turn to the door, and emerge into the new world order I have created.

I kicked the hornets' nest, they will swarm me.

Stepping out of the staff toilet I run into Peter McNeil and almost fall to the ground. He grabs my arm and puts me back on my feet. I try to walk away but he steps right in front of me.

"You're not staff. That's a detention." Taking out his detention book he flips to a new page. "Where are you supposed to be right now?"

"Maths, van Zyl." Let him write me up, he'll find he's last in a long queue.

"I'll put you down for tomorrow, unless you have a great reason why I shouldn't?" He waits, pencil in hand, blue eyes filled with amusement like someone enjoying the antics of a misbehaving three-year-old.

I taste salt on my lips. The auto-pilot tears are back. He pulls a huge, white tissue from his trouser pocket and presses it into my hand. It smells of incense. Why does he need scented tissues? Does he think girls like them that way?

"Okay, July, stop, no need for that. Forget the detention. Genuinely, this is not a big deal, nothing worth crying over.

Are you hurt?"

I take the tissue and blow my nose. I'm not sick. I'm broken in an unfixable place.

"Let's go and find help. Mrs Prince in the office is nice." He hands me another tissue. I dab my chin to stop the waterfall dripping onto my shirt collar.

"Shall we go?" he asks.

"No," I answer, walking away. He follows, persistent like his little brother.

"Jackie's in the prefects' room if you want to talk to someone. No one else is there. You'd have the place to yourselves."

"No." This time he lets me go.

Mr van Zyl ignores my late arrival. I'm not a troublemaker and my grades are good. I take out my books and notice a spot of blood on my boot. I wipe it with my finger. David is watching me. A huge, white, unscented tissue arrives on my desk. I feel my face. It's still wet. I nod my thanks. He shrugs, still mad at me. He doesn't know about Andie.

The school lockdown alarm flashes. Mr van Zyl bolts the door and we all sit on the floor under our desks. I hear police sirens and an ambulance chasing up the hill.

Leyton's been found.

10. REVELATION

I'M HALFWAY DOWN THE DRIVE following a group of grade eight boys when David McNeil steps out from the trees and starts walking beside me. Again I'm disappointed in myself for not having noticed him. I'll never survive this war this way.

"Hey, have you decided on the Andie thing?" He fakes moderate interest.

I put him out of his misery. "Andie is home."

"How do you know?" He comes closer and his eyes bore down on me. I speed up, forgetting he has longer legs than me.

"Is she okay?" he demands.

"No. She was raped." I speak to the air in front of me and keep moving.

He walks six paces before my words sink in. Then he grabs my arm. I freeze, shake off his hand. He lets go. I start walking. He's next to me like a persistent fly.

"Who did it?" he asks. I stop. He stops.

"Who? That's easy . . . a male. Like you. One of your kind. You!"

He is outraged. "Hey! Don't you blame me, not that. Not me."

I step in front of him now, making him stop. "Definitely you, you and your kind don't stop the rapists among you. You cover for them. You talk about girls as boobs, bums, and honey pots, just body parts, not people, not human beings, not worthy of respect or kindness, then you disown the consequences. You, and I mean *you*, you are definitely to blame."

"I didn't do anything. Anyway, who found her? Is she at home?"

"After the party, you missed your curfew, why?" I ask. His own words mark him as a boy who doesn't take responsibility for his own actions. I want to know who he is blaming this time.

"How do you know about that?"

"I listen. Why did you miss your curfew?" I start walking, I have a bus to catch. He follows.

"Lucas du Toit offered me a lift home. He's Leigh-Anne's brother and a cop. I thought he'd use every back road, ignore speed limits, and get me home early, but he filled his car with his sister and her friends and took them home first. That's why I got in after midnight."

Like an earworm, I hear Andie mumbling, "Luke, Luke, Luke . . . " My brain sparks. I follow the light and find a hot coal. What if she was actually saying "Lucas," as in Lucas du Toit? A policeman connected to Blue Ridge College through his sister. The police have total freedom to get around with no one watching them. As the Law, wearing police blues, this Lucas could pretend to help his victims while actually committing crimes and covering his tracks. Is he the rapist I'm looking for?

I study David. How innocent is this sample of the principal's sperm?

"Why did you trust this cop?"

"His sister's good friends with my brother."

"She likes to swim in a crowded pool."

He laughs. "Yes, he has it sweet. What will Andie do now? What happens now?"

"Did you tell your tame policeman about your curfew?"

"No, from Mark's place to here is about ten minutes. I had to be home by twelve. I got in the car just after ten-thirty. Why would I be late?"

"People can't read your mind, you know."

"Wish they could. It would make life a lot easier."

We reach the turning to the narrow road down to his home.

"Bye," he says. I nod and catch up to the grade eight boys heading to the bus stop.

If Lucas du Toit is my target I need to find him and check him out. If I follow Leigh-Anne she might lead me to him, but I only know her as Peter McNeil's air-headed, arm candy. The office will have her file. I can get her address there.

A white car pulls up to the bus stop. Andre Vermarck leans out the passenger window.

"Hey, July! See you at home!" He laughs and the car speeds off.

Andre Vermarck, best friend of Leyton Donaldson, and member of Richter's inner circle. He sold me the dagga for my mom, all compassion and understanding, until last Friday when he handed me to the rapist.

I wait until the car disappears around the curve at Loftus Versveld then run back into the school grounds and sprint up the steep forest track to the only fortress I have; the school's sickroom.

Branches whip my face, thorns tug at my clothes. My lungs are on fire, sweat clouds my sight.

"Hide in the paint shed, darling. I love you," I hear Mom say.

The paint shed stands in a small alcove in the forest below the school building. I pull open the metal door and step inside. Tins stacked on brick-and-wood shelving line the walls. Larger tins cover the floor. The place reeks of paint and turpentine. I find a 5L tin near the back and sit down. My legs throb. I'm still heaving for breath.

None of it matters. I heard Mom. I am officially mad.

Ghosts. Spirits. The dead. All words that mean distance, a divide, definitely far away, but I heard her voice, felt her breath on my cheek as she spoke.

My mother is dead; and the dead live on the other side of vision and can't talk to you or hug you or scare you shitless by whispering warm words in your ear.

I've never watched a ghost movie. Mom said real life made horror movies pale into insignificance, and she knew because she worked in casualty at Tshwane District Hospital, amidst the blood and gore that lubricate the thin edge of life.

As a recent entry into the Dead Relatives club, I don't know enough about communication between the invisible and the visible. Maybe ghostly encounters happen all the time, but those in the club don't mention them to outsiders in case they find the proximity of free-range dead people upsetting. Perhaps rules keep the dead in fixed zones around their own living. I imagine invisible traffic lights, yellow lines indicating dividing zones, parking lanes for those squashed out of their own zones by the presence of others, and ghostly traffic cops wielding orange light batons.

While alive, Mom searched for bible stories about the afterlife. She enjoyed the one about Lazarus and the rich man.

"Look, July, the rich man can see Lazarus and talk to him, and Lazarus can hear him. That proves it, communication can happen. When I'm in heaven I'll be able to hear you. I'll ask Jesus to let me come back to you," she said once and sat back with a deep contented sigh.

With Mom here I relax. Warm in my big jacket, I close my eyes and imagine going home, Mom peeling potatoes and singing in the kitchen, the savory fragrance of a chicken casserole in the oven, the front door closed tight against the world.

Down from the school, the Dutch Reformed Church bell tolls five o'clock. Mr Labuschagne locks the school at six on a Monday evening.

Mom stands guard. I am safe. I lean back against the wall of tins and fall asleep.

11. BEHIND THE BIKE SHED

I OPEN MY EYES TO TOTAL DARKNESS and fall off the paint can. The smell returns my memory. Feeling my way to the door, I step out into the crisp air. Moonshine deepens and multiplies the shadows in the forest. Feeling confident now, I amble up to the school building.

Someone is jogging up the driveway, panting hard. From a hidden spot I watch the boy. He turns in at the swimming pool enclosure and starts sprinting up and down the steps leading down to the pool. I've never counted them but there are a lot. After swimming, I can barely drag myself up all of them to get back to the change rooms. I think the lunatic is David McNeil. It makes sense, this is his home turf.

I'm about to continue up to the school when I spot two other boys walking up the narrow service road that leads from the west entrance gate, and ends at the Industrial Arts Centre. Students aren't allowed on the service road, but I know Richter's gang use it. He keeps a brown Ford Transit van in the courtyard of the Industrial Arts Centre. Not hidden, or covered, out for everyone to see. Until I bought hash from Andre Vermarck, I thought the students in the mechanic classes used the van for their hands-on lessons, but now I know it is Richter's drug stockroom. It shows even the teachers are scared of him.

Did Andre Vermarck, discovering I'm not at home, send these boys to find me?

Keeping to the forest paths, I run down to the west side of

the school and hide behind the bike shed in the courtyard of
the Industrial Arts Centre.

David McNeil appears around the corner. He stops close
enough for me to whisper, "Very quietly and slowly take cover
behind the bike rack."

He jumps as though he's stepped on a live wire. The back
of the bike rack stands close to the school wall, with a narrow
space between. It has a solid metal back board two metres wide
and about a metre high. David backs up and begins to fold
his six-foot-two frame next to me. It's like watching a Great
Dane climb through a cat flap, with the accompanying grunts
and yelps. I place my finger on my lips to shush him. He nods
and freezes, holding his breath. His clothes are drenched with
sweat, his arms are sticky, and he's dripping and pressed up tight
against my side. I turn my face away and breathe through my
mouth.

Travis Richter and Andre Vermarck approach the van, the
wide beams of their flashlights bobbing. Richter is as thin as
a snake, Vermarck the muscled enforcer. Both wear black and
carry bulging backpacks. Richter unlocks the rear doors of the
vehicle and swings them open. They place the backpacks in the
van.

Richter's talking, " . . . and the party this Friday is at the
contact's place. It's a plot. South. We're doing it alone." He pulls
small white bags out of his backpack and stacks them in the
van.

Tossing Vermarck some keys, he goes on, "Get the scale out
the safe. We need to check these are kosher."

"The Du Toit place?" Vermarck asks climbing inside the
van. "That's way on the other side of Rooihuiskraal—no, even
further, it's out Mnandi way. Isn't that Rivonia? Why go there?"
He hands Richter the scale and jumps out the van.

"We don't have an option. It's where he wants to meet and I

have to fix the shit you started. I need this guy." Richter places
a white bag on the scales. "He's the gate into the big pond. Pass
me the next bag, start from the left."

"He's happy. Why change?"

"Not so fast. I'm still thinking," Richter replies, weighing
each of the packets and noting the results on the bags with a
black marker pen. "We deal in this stuff. This is our bread and
butter, our sure thing. Why risk it all? This other business with
girls, what do we know about it? It's better to know what you
do, and do what you know."

"And do who you know," Vermarck quips. Richter doesn't
laugh.

"On Friday, Mpho will drive. I'll take care of the deal.
Leyton will act as decoy, you're lookout."

"If Leyton can," Vermarck says.

"True. I might need a backup."

They work steadily, emptying both backpacks.

Richter locks the van.

"Does Leigh-Anne know about the contact?" Vermarck asks.
They walk past the bike shed. David and I hold our breath.

"She doesn't act like she does, and we'll keep it that way."
Richter leads the way across the driveway and onto the grass.
"We'll go this way to avoid McNeil's house. I thought I heard
something earlier this evening."

They switch on their flashlights and disappear into the forest.

I wait another five minutes in case they forget something
and come back.

David whispers into my ear, "Hey, July. They've gone. Can
we move? I'm dying here."

Pulling my coat tightly around me, I stand up and slide out
from behind the bike shed, still keeping an eye on the forest
and the van.

He swivels sideways, stretches out his legs and groans in pain.

"Both my legs are totally numb." He sneezes three times in a row. "By the way you smell of paint and turpentine."

"You stink of sweat."

He grins sheepishly "True. How did you know they were here?"

"Fell over them and you within minutes."

Standing up he limps from foot to foot like a dancing bear. I don't laugh, it would encourage him to linger and I want him gone so I can barrier myself in my fortress and be safely alone. Then, maybe Mom will come and we can talk. My chest aches with a new sharp pain. It must be the part that she occupies; it's hungry for her to come home.

David says, "I can't believe they're hiding their drugs right here at the school. How can they get away with it?" He walks over to the van, tries its doors. Locked. "That thing is always parked here. I thought it was used by the Industrial Arts classes. It has no right to be here."

He hobbles around in front of me, supposedly stretching his muscles, but I think it keeps the tiny wheels in his brain rotating which then activates his mouth. One thing I know about David McNeil is that he doesn't shift easily. I stay by the shed. Someone might arrive to drive the loaded van away.

"Well, tell your daddy to fix it. I bet he knows about Richter and his gang. If he doesn't, then he's blind and dumb."

He comes beside me. "What did they mean about the girls? That's what they said, isn't it?"

"Yes, that's what they said."

"But we need to stop them!" Conviction sharpens his tone. "They could be the guys who raped Andie." He stares expectantly at me.

"Yes they could be, but I'm not taking on the Richter gang. You can. You have more friends than me. Perhaps a rugby team can take down a drug gang. Give it a go."

He thinks about that. "Not me. I'm grounded after the last party." He frowns and stares at me. "Anyhow, what are you doing here this late at night? There are no activities now."

"Saving your butt."

He blushes deep red. I hit a nerve.

"You're too late for that," he says and blushes again. "Don't your parents worry about you being out this late?"

"My mother knows where I am."

"I can take you home." He looks around at the dark school buildings and the forest. "As we've just seen, this place is not safe."

"No. I'm fine. You go on. Your folks will be missing you."

"I'm not going home tonight." He stops himself, regretting his words. Then I remember what I did to him. A tickle of guilt activates my conscience.

"Those Intervention slips?"

"You heard?" He looks away, embarrassed; swipes his fringe off his face.

"The whole school did. Everyone talks when a new record is set. There are bets out there to see if you can sit down tomorrow. Because rumour has it your dad canes you. But I've seen you in action, I'm changing my bet. I think you will."

"You think you've seen me in action?" he asks with a sour laugh. "No! What you saw was me not wanting to die. Without the fear of death hanging over my head, I don't think I can sit down. Yes my dad caned me. I'll even give you the stats: six for the three Intervention slips and four for insubordination. Now you're up to date. Spread it around. Keep your bet. I don't want to cost you money." He takes three steps away from me then stops. "Sorry. I shouldn't blast you. It's not your fault. Let me get you home safely. I can't leave you here."

"I'm fine. Where will you spend the night?" I am actually interested.

"I haven't decided. I'll get you home first." He holds out his arm as if to guide me down the aisle. I laugh, shake my head, and speak slowly like to a small child,

"Please go away. I am fine."

But he doesn't go, he asks, "Do you like Mango Groove?"

"Yes. Go home." I'm getting frustrated with his stalling.

"Great! 'Dance Some More' and 'Special Star' are the best. They make you want to dance." He grins at me. I'm about to speak when I hear shouting. I whisper,

"Shhh, someone's coming up the driveway." I move away from him. He mustn't see me go inside the building. He follows me. I ask, "Is your dad searching for you? I think they are calling your name."

He listens and swallows hard, his Adams apple working up and down. He wipes the sweat out of his eyes. "Yes, that's him. What do I do?" He hugs himself and studies the ground. "I can't take any more."

I whisper, "You're free to run away. Take the forest path behind the Centre. Chris will take you in."

He gives me a forced smile. "I know, but isn't that the coward's way out? I caused this, I pay the price."

Stepping closer to him, I say, "Your choice. Your fight. I'm gone. Don't mention me." While he looks down the driveway, I step under the archway to the north quad's gate, unlock it, and slip inside while he concentrates on his father's arrival. At least I know I'm still safe in the school.

12. TUESDAY INVITATION

AT FIRST BREAK, I walk to the east quad and sit down against the brick wall in the corridor opposite the staffroom windows. The stone floor below me is cold but the sunshine is warm. Staff and prefects alike ignore me. Mom hasn't spoken to me again. I want her to.

I've heard nothing about Leyton since the ambulance carted him off. I'm not surprised. Blue Ridge College never allows bad publicity. It markets itself as a luxury yacht of interracial harmony on the rough South African seas. Even one crack in its hull and the super rich will vanish with their money and their children.

Which prompts a disturbing thought: Blue Ridge is expensive, where did Mom get the money to send me here? Is Mr Stedman paying my fees? Maybe the school even sends him copies of my reports. I feel exposed, like I've found a drill hole in my bedroom wall. Who will tell me the truth about him? He creeps me out.

Mom put me here because she wanted the best for me. Knowing better now, is she feeling guilty? I mutter, "Don't worry Mom, the worst that can happen is I get up there with you faster than you expected." She knows that getting her dagga led to my rape. Can you be upset in heaven? If you can, I think she is pacing heaven, knocking on the door of Management to find out what can be done. On Earth, more dedicated than a terrier after a bone, she made things happen. She'll be the same up there.

I did look up Leigh-Anne du Toit on an office computer. Her parents are divorced. She lives in Brooklyn with her mother. No help to me, because her brother, Lucas, lives out in a distant place called Mnandi. It's not on any Pretoria bus route. I don't have access to a car. Perhaps I can find the police station where he works. Then again, I mustn't narrow my suspect list too soon. Lucas might be a diversion.

Khetiwe and Lily stroll together into the quad. They look around, spot me, and head straight over. I am instantly on my guard. Do they know I spied on them or that I put Andie in the stranger's car? They sit down on either side of me and I feel trapped.

"Here you are," Khetiwe says as if ending a game of hide-and-seek. "We've been looking all over for you. Don't you usually go to the Media Centre? Anyway, not important, we found you." She seems very pleased with herself. Rumour has it she is Zulu royalty. Blue blood makes her stick up her nose at everyone. I'm surprised she knows my name.

"We want to ask you a question," Lily says setting a more serious tone.

Lily is a sweet Maltese poodle and Khetiwe her hungry caracal friend. However much you want to pat the Maltese you know the caracal will savage your outstretched arm. Andie was the spaniel in the group; dewy eyes, floppy ears, and cute.

Lily continues, "We think you're the exact right person to help us find out who attacked Andie."

I avoid eye contact and study the windows in the wall opposite me.

"You see," Khetiwe adds, "if we know who he is, we can stay away from him. So will you help us? No one has to know." She nods at me like the deal is done; she speaks and I obey. Did I mention Khetiwe has bright red hair that she wears in a big round bubble? She's as inconspicuous as a fire engine. Lily has blue eyes, long, braided blonde hair, pale skin; boys dance around her like bees around a hive.

"No. Thank you." Staying alive takes all my time, I don't need these two added to my worries.

"Please, July, just hear us out," Lily says. "We are in danger, you are too. We need you."

She's got a point. I'm alone, and alone means vulnerable. They say there is safety in numbers. I need a group. If you're walking in a direction and someone walks with you, you have company; maybe not a friend, but still, company. If a lion appears and you run the fastest, the lion eats the company. I ask,

"You have lots of other friends, why me specifically?"

"You get around a lot and meet all types of people . . . people we don't know," Khetiwe says.

"Don't believe the rumours," I retort.

Khetiwe flicks at her hair and says airily, "Well you live in Sunnyside, that's a very cosmopolitan suburb, all those tall blocks of flats."

"If you mean poor, then that's true, but how does that help you?"

"Well, among all those people you've probably seen some rapists," Khetiwe says. "You can tell us what they look like."

There must be an -ism that describes people who despise the poor—wealthism, poorism. I don't know, but an example of one is standing in front of me. I'm not ashamed of being poor or of living in Sunnyside. I stand up, collect my bag, and walk down the corridor.

Like marionettes on a string, they rise with me. Lily at least looks ashamed, but Khetiwe rolls her eyes and says, "It's the truth. Facts are facts. No need to get all hot and bothered."

"Let's talk facts, Khetiwe," I slam back. "Sexual predators inhabit every income level. Rape is an attitude not an income statement. Anyway, why ask me? You were there with Andie at

Mark's place. If anyone knows what happened to her, it's you."

She reacts as if I slapped her. "Me? I didn't see who took her. Why would I be here if I did?"

"You tell me. Why are you?" I pull up and look her directly in the eye.

Startled, she huffs and puffs like a steam engine, at a loss for words.

I notice Richter's pet cobra, Mpho Kageso, shadow-blending in the passage to south quad. I'll have to walk right past him. He's medium height with dark hair and complexion. He attacks if confronted but mostly he spies.

"Wait! Stop!" Lily places her hand on my arm. "You give us his name, we tell the police, they'll arrest him, and we'd all be safe again."

I pull my arm free of her. "You are twice wrong. I don't know any rapists, and the police won't do anything."

"Rubbish," Khetiwe says. "My father told me they are already investigating Andie's case."

"Good. Then go and ask him." I put the girls between me and Kageso and get through the archway.

"We want to speed things up," Lily says. "Don't you even know what one looks like?"

I look at Lily and think of her brother, Grant, a prefect. He fits the bill exactly: blond hair, blue eyes, white.

"He looks like your brother, Lily. Your dad's a big-shot judge. Ask him what a rapist looks like. He must have seen at least one." We're in the south quad. I'm safe.

She glares at me. "My brother isn't a rapist and my father doesn't talk to me about his cases."

"They should. They both know more rapists than I do."

"We just want to protect ourselves. Why won't you help us?" Khetiwe says. "We want to feel safe. What do we do if he shows up?"

I open my mouth to answer and hear myself say, "Scream, fight, bite, kick. If you have a weapon cut off his balls; blind him; crush his kneecaps; break his hands!"

They look shocked. I smile. Releasing my pent-up rage felt great. I think my smile pushes them over the top, now they believe I'm unhinged as well as poor.

Lily pulls on Khetiwe's arm. "We should go. Thank you, July. We'll think about what you said."

They flee down the cloister. I'm glad. It's easier to keep secrets when you're working alone.

There's a bench outside my next class and I sit down for the last five minutes of break.

In a flash of blue blazer and grey flannel, Andre Vermarck sits down beside me. He stinks of cigarette smoke. Something hard pokes into my side—not a knife but a small hand gun. I'm terrified. Is this it, finally? I look around but no one pays us any attention. My mouth is so dry I can't croak let alone scream.

"Listen up, bitch. Time's up. You don't stick one of us and walk away. No ways. Say your prayers. You're done."

He gets up as abruptly as he sat down, and hooking the gun into the back of his belt like a thug in an American cop show he leaves.

I float high above my body. The bell rings. My body walks into the accounting class.

13. ACCOUNTING

THE WHOLE SCHOOL IS TALKING about David. They know his father beat the shit out of him last night. They didn't hear it from me. I didn't tell them because, well, his pain is totally my creation. Betting on his sitting time is fast and competitive. The current time to beat is 33 seconds. I didn't take out a bet because it didn't seem fair. I'm impressed with David's stoicism. He's tolerant, he grins, and he acts as if it's a normal everyday occurrence.

Unfortunately for him, accounting sinks into a gong show. It's the only class where he has to sit right in the front. All eyes are glued to his backside. Mark has a stopwatch and loudly clicks on it every time David sits down, and clicks it off when David eases his bum off the seat by leaning forward on his elbows. There is laughter and applause. Chris announces the time and distributes the winnings.

Mrs Rayton likes balance. She hates disorder. She also hates David. His grade average is F minus. The effort he puts into accounting wouldn't produce a fart even if he'd eaten a can of beans. She takes this personally. Tracking the source of the unrest, she glares through her thick glasses at David.

"Enough! Silence! Sit down, David. I can't see those behind you. Who is causing the commotion?"

"Yes, sit down David, you make the place look untidy," Mark says stoking the crowd.

"Yeah, sit—you make a better door than a window," Chris says grinning widely.

Mrs Rayton glares at them then returns to David, the focus of the disturbance. She's a cat playing with a wounded bird. It makes me uncomfortable.

"David? Is there a problem?" She taps on his desk with her pen.

"No, ma'am." He's sitting down but his face is flushed.

"If you disturb my class one more time, for whatever reason, I will send you straight to the office. Do you understand?"

He nods. "Yes, ma'am."

His friends all chuckle and Mrs Rayton is about to explode. I'm surprised David can sit at all. What kind of people are we if we laugh at someone in pain instead of offering help?

I lift up my boot-encased feet and clunk them onto my desk and start undoing the laces. I flick them left and right while muttering gibberish.

"Oh no!" Mrs Rayton runs down the aisle to me. "No, July, we don't do that in this school. We keep our boots on and our feet on the floor. Do NOT take your boots off. NO!"

I pull off my left boot, upend it and tap it to see if anything comes out. A little sand. Then I take off my right boot. Khauhelo pulls a face at me and sprays deodorant into the air. Taking her cue, the others hold their noses, pretend to choke, and rush to the open windows.

Mrs Rayton bounces up and down with frustration. "If you do not put on your boots I will send you to the office."

The sand in my right boot forms a tiny pile on the floor.

"Out. Immediately. Out now!" Mrs Rayton shouts, pulling at my arm. "Straight to the office. Consider yourself automatically on detention!"

I pull myself free of her and finish cleaning my boots. It takes me a while to put them on and tie up the laces. She watches me, arms crossed, face crimson with fury. I leave, pausing only to wink at David as I pass. He nods his thanks.

I make my way to the Media Centre, sit down in one of the comfy chairs in the magazine area, and pick up an issue of *Science for Today*. A tear drops on the page; my eyes are leaking. Searching my pockets for a tissue, I find a note. It reads, "Meet us in the Media Centre at 2ndB K & L."

They are persistent and I need company. I'll listen to their plans.

14. THE DEAL

THE MEDIA CENTRE FILLS up with students at break because it's warm. Khetiwe and Lily walk right past me and go to the encyclopedia section where they sit down at the long table. I get up and move to a bookcase behind them to listen in. I need to know why they want to involve me. Whose side are they on?

"She's nuts," Khetiwe says. "Not even bush nuts. I'm talking fallen-off-the-bush and rotting-on-the-ground nuts. If she finds him for us and maims him, we'll go to jail as accomplices. I don't think we should be doing this. Let's find someone else."

"Who? I've spoken to my brothers and they keep saying I need to stay home and take care. Not, 'cut off his balls' like July says. She's the one we need. Have you seen how even yucky boys like Kevin Abbot steer clear of her? Whatever she does to keep them scared, I want it."

"I've never heard you sound so passionate about anything. You really want to nail this guy."

"Yes, I do, for us and for Andie. We'll listen to July and take baby steps. If we decide to bail out halfway, we can."

Because of Lily, I go and sit down at their table. They jump.

"How did you get in?" Khetiwe demands. "I've been watching that door like I'm expecting pizza delivery."

"I'm here now. Listen up, whatever you have to say you can't do it here, not with all these Matrics flapping their long ears our way. I'm going to a safer spot. If you want to talk follow me. If not, stay here."

"It's cold out there," Khetiwe says with a shiver.

"Your choice, I'm gone." I thread my way through the crowd and out the door, giving a brief nod to David, who's standing at the magazine rack reading a *History Today*.

The wind is icy. Antarctic air over Cape Town has dropped snow on the Cape Fold Mountains, sending frigid air rolling northwards up and across the plateau to chill Pretoria. Few students hang about outside.

I lead Khetiwe and Lily to the sheltered grassy courtyard between the gym and the tuck shop and make straight for the metal bench under the large oak tree in the centre. Here I know no one will sneak up on us. I sit down and indicate to the girls to do likewise.

"Ugh, July, we'll get into trouble if we're found here. They'll think we're smokers," Khetiwe says, easing herself down onto the bench as if it were crawling with fire ants. "This bench is freezing." She toes a pile of cigarette butts. "It's disgusting here."

"But no one can get close enough to listen in." I kick some butts out of the way and see David watching us from the corner. On the pool steps sits Vermarck. We are under strict observation. I can hear the seconds of my life ticking away.

Lily stares at the butts and wrinkles her nose. "Some look like they have blood on them. Yuck! They're filthy. The people on detention are supposed to do clean-up chores. I'm going to speak to Grant. He needs to fix this."

"You can get HIV from saliva, and even the tiniest fleck of blood," Khetiwe says, glaring at me, as if I'm personally responsible for the disease.

"Then don't eat them. Talk, but keep your voices down."

Lily says, "We want you to help us find the rapist."

Khetiwe nods agreement. "Forget the police. We'll hand his

name to our parents: Mr Elliott, Lily's father, or mine. They'll fix him one shot."

"No, they won't," I reply. "They'll hand him to the police and nothing will change."

"Then we'll tell everyone we know," Lily says. "Spread the word and force him to move."

"That's not fair," I say. "Chasing him away to an area where the girls don't know about him."

Khetiwe rolls her eyes at me. I stare her down. She fluffs her hair with her fingers. "Look—will you help us or not? Just say yes or no, I don't want to sit here freezing to death if you still won't help."

"What are you hoping I can do?" I am torn, extra bodies will protect me, but a secret shared is not a secret any more and I have secrets.

"Tell us where to start," Lily says, eyes shining with enthusiasm.

"We can pay you," Khetiwe says. "Or if there's something else you want, we will do what we can to get it for you."

I let all my wants flash through my mind: to be unraped, for Mom to be undead, for life to be unweird, to be unalone. Imagine if Khetiwe and Lily waved all that away with one stroke of a credit card. Thinking about it overwhelms me with longing for my old life where my biggest worry was pimples on my forehead.

"Okay, but if we search for the rapist together we play by my rules. That's the deal."

"What are your rules?" Lily asks, ever cautious.

"No talking about this to anyone outside of this group. Playing it totally safe, not being heroes. We want him to go down not us. Lots of planning and research before we do anything; the guy is ruthless."

"And your payment? What do you want?" Khetiwe asks, her

tone sharp like she expects me to overcharge and under-provide.

"We'll talk about that later, if we get to that point." This is my team, but if I had a choice, never in a million years would I have chosen these two girls.

"Oh, I know something I wanted to tell you," Lily says. "My brother, Grant, told me last night that Leigh-Anne du Toit is having a party this Friday at her brother's place in Mnandi. If the rapist tries again, he might do it there."

"And Lily's older brother, Darren, will go because he is friends with Leigh-Anne's brother, Lucas," Khetiwe says. "So we can all hitch a ride."

And there goes my team, fallen at the first post. I will not help these girls. Imagine all my information handed straight to the man I strongly suspect is the rapist. They are not my team, but they are my cover. They will get me close to my target. I must hang on to them.

Lily nods. "We'll be safe with Darren there. He's in his final year of law at Wits. Next year he joins my father's firm to work for his Articles."

"You two really do want to do this, don't you?" I say. They nod. "It's going to be far more dangerous than sitting in Smokers' Corner. You could get hurt."

"Not at this party," Khetiwe says. "Not with Darren there, and Leigh-Anne's brother is a cop. That's why it's a good one to start on. Who's going to crash it? And most of Leigh-Anne's friends are prefects, and most of their boyfriends are already out of school. With all those law-abiding adults around, it will be really safe."

"Except for the rapist," I say. "Never underestimate your enemy."

"Do you think I should ask Grant to come as well?" Lily asks. "To build up our numbers."

"As long as you remember you can't tell them what we're

actually doing. Don't forget my first rule," I remind them. "No talking about this to anyone outside this group."

"I know. I won't." Lily's expression is sober. She understands how serious this is. Khetiwe, on the other hand, looks spaced out.

"If we don't find him this Friday, that's it, I'm out," she says. "I don't keep secrets from my mother."

"Baby steps," Lily says, smiling. "We edge forward tiny bit by tiny bit and stop when we want to."

"Forget baby steps!" I say. "If this man we're hunting hears about this plan, he's going to take us down, and he enjoys hurting and raping girls. He's already proven that. Imagine yourself caught alone with him. How will you fight back? You need weapons."

"Stop it, July," Lily says. "You're making it sound worse than it will be. This Friday we'll be with friends."

"Not all of them. If we're going ahead you need to prepare for the worst. From now on, carry pepper spray, a fully charged and operational mobile phone, and a knife."

"Say that again?" Lily asks taking out a small notebook and pen. Khetiwe watches. She still feels far away, uninvolved. It makes me uneasy. If she speaks of this meeting the danger level on my life goes from red to nuclear fireball mushroom cloud. For my safety she must stay with us.

I repeat, "Pepper spray, mobiles, knives, and a finger in each eye will also work wonders." I lunge two fingers at Lily's face ending two millimetres from her eyes. She flinches, eyes wide in alarm. I say, "Lily, slap my hand away. Do it. Slap my hand." Instead of cowering I need her to fight back.

She laughs at me and looks around the quad. "Don't be silly, people are watching."

"Khetiwe," I ask. "Do you have a weapon?"

"Not yet. I'll buy it all this afternoon at the Mall. You'll come with me, Lily?"

The bell rings.

Khetiwe stands up and brushes off her skirt. "July, we forgot to mention another part of the deal: you have to be with us wherever we go, starting with this Friday's party. If you need a lift we'll take you there." She smiles. When caracals smile it doesn't mean they want to hug you, it means you're supper.

She doesn't trust me. The feeling is mutual and I have more to lose. "I'll be there but I'm not your bodyguard. You must protect yourselves."

They follow me back to the main path, as do my observers.

"I need the loo. See you in class." I leave them and walk through the north gate. I want to know why David is watching me.

He walks behind me into geography and whispers, "The Richter gang is tracking you."

"I know," I reply.

"Why?" he says in surprise. "What did you do?"

"I was born female. As for you—stop spying on me. Everyone notices when one of the principal's sons acts weird. Don't feed the rumour mill. Do you want your dad hearing that we've been hanging out together behind the bike shed?"

He blushes bright pink. "But—well that wasn't—okay, I get it. I just wanted to say thanks for accounting. I owe you one."

"Jeez, your maths is putrid. You owe me two, and fair warning, I might take you up on them." I walk towards my desk. If the whole school knows Richter is watching me, then I am safer than before; too many eyes cancel out a secret attack.

15. PHONE CALL

WEDNESDAY MORNING, HALF WAY through mathematics, the intercom springs to life. "July Abraham, July Abraham, please come to the main office immediately. July Abraham, please come to the main office." Everyone turns to stare at me. I have so many sins I wonder which I'm being called on.

"Out you go," Mr van Zyl says. "Don't forget your homework."

Mrs Prince is waiting for me at the counter. "It's a phone call. Come to my desk and take it there." She opens the security door and lets me through. I sit at her desk and pick up the phone. Mrs Prince goes back to the counter to give me privacy.

"Hello? July here," I whisper.

"July, sorry to phone you at school," Mrs Gresham sounds caring and efficient. "I haven't forgotten my promise, but I need to ask you a couple of questions about your mom's funeral tomorrow. I'll collect you from school at two-thirty. Is that still okay, Sweetie? Do you have something smart to wear? I can bring you a dress and things if you don't."

The phone is heavy in my hand. My throat constricts. I close my eyes to block out the school office. If my two worlds collide I will be ripped apart. I don't have enough strength to carry a double weight.

Licking my lips, I select words that if overheard won't give away my secret. My mother is dead.

"Yes, thank you. I'll wait right outside the main doors. If you have something suitable I'll wear it. How long will it all take?"

"The church service is about an hour. I don't know how many people will show up. Anyone can come to a funeral. I didn't put it in the paper, your mom said not to tell anyone, but the people who know her will come. After, there's the wake in the church hall: sandwiches, coffee, and tea. We won't attend. We'll head straight to the crematorium."

"Will you take me home afterwards?" I ask, forgetting my flat is compromised.

"Yes, if that's what you want, but why not stay with me. You'll be tired after the day."

"Okay. I'll do that. Thank you for phoning. See you tomorrow. Bye."

I replace the phone and look for Mrs Prince.

"Everything okay, love?" she asks.

"Yes, thank you," I reply, but the ground sways beneath me like a rope bridge across a canyon. Mom is dead. My life up to that point has been wiped away and I don't know if I get a Part Two. Then there's that unknown father. I push him to the back of my mind. If I rip into any more parts I'll cease to exist.

The bell for second break must have rung while I was in the office. I grab my bag from the empty classroom and find a note stuck to it. It reads: Second break. SC. K&L.

Mpho Kageso leans against the wall of Smoker's Corner watching Khetiwe and Lily sitting on the bench under the oak tree.

I approach them. "We're being watched. Let's go to the east quad."

Lily smiles at me and holds out a paper bag. "I stopped at the tuck shop and bought you a jam donut to cheer you up. You've looked sad all day. Do you want to talk about it?"

With a lump in my throat, I take the bag and sit down on the edge of the bench. "No. Thank you. We really have to move. If you look left you'll see Mpho Kageso watching us. That's not a good thing. You'll become targets." They look but don't move.

Khetiwe leans across Lily and places a package on my lap. "If we have to sit out here we can all keep warm."

Lily adds, "All in legal school blue. Open it."

Inside there are a scarf and a pair of gloves. Lily and Khetiwe giggle and put theirs on, and Lily, noticing my dumbfounded surprise, wraps the scarf around my neck and pushes the gloves on to my hands.

"There, now, we can meet anywhere and not freeze to death." She sits back satisfied.

While the clothing provides physical warmth, knowing they thought of me, noticed me as a person when I wasn't with them, starts a blaze that radiates to every part of my being. I bite back tears. Mom always dropped a box of Smarties or a Kit-Kat into her shopping basket to give me when she got home; it showed she never stopped thinking about me. If these girls care, like it seems they do, I need to see them as real people and not rich people.

"Thanks. Thank you, both. I still think we should move." Again they ignore me and move in closer.

Lily whispers, "We went into that big weapons store in Menlyn and bought knives. What an amazing place. Oh my . . . I loved it. I will be going back." Her eyes shine with excitement.

"What did you buy?" I ask, unsettled by her enthusiasm.

"Chisel-sharp, fifteen-degree grind, ten-centimetre folding blade," Lily says. "The shop guy was very helpful. He said we needed a working knife, small and sharp." She holds out a shiny maroon switchblade. "This fits the bill. We both got the same type."

"An elegant weapon," I say, taking it and flicking it open.

"Balanced, light, but with weight. What can you do with it?" I give it back and she receives it in two hands like it's made of the finest china.

Khetiwe answers, "The guy at the weapons shop said to half defrost some thick steaks and try getting the knife in and slicing down. We already tried it. We also tried with gristle. Tell us what else to do and we'll work on it."

Lily balances her knife on the tip of her pointer finger, fascinated by her acquisition.

"We used that human anatomy diagram in our biology books and practiced finding the vital organs on each other," she says. "Then, taking Grant's skeleton, we worked out how to get past the rib bones. They really do decide where you can put in the blade."

I visualize the two of them in pink-pillowed, heart-mirrored bedrooms, practicing lethal strokes, while down in a soap-opera style lounge their mothers sit drinking lemon tea from bone china cups. Guilt strikes. I don't want to turn them into killers or get them killed. I've gone too far. I have to stop this.

"It's not a game. You could be hurt, or killed. The rapist likes to hurt girls. I don't think you've ever had someone hurt you." I can't share my nightmare. It still won't squash down into any existing words.

"We know it's going to be dangerous," Khetiwe says. "That's why we're working at getting it right." Her knife has a pearl handle. It matches her long, decorated finger nails.

"We won't use our knives unless we have to," Lily says, putting hers back in her pocket.

"Andie's dad's got a transfer down to Pietermaritzburg," Khetiwe says. "They move as soon as they can find a house. She's been accepted at Epworth. It's an all girls' private boarding school. She said she'll feel safe there. Listening to her breaks my heart. She sounds hollow."

"We can stop that happening again. That's what we can do," Lily says.

The bell rings. Lily walks next to me and takes my arm. I accept her support.

"Don't worry July, We're strong together."

I want to believe her.

16. THURSDAY AFTERNOON

I'M ON THE SCHOOL STEPS waiting for Mrs Gresham to take me to Mom's funeral. I've never been to a funeral. What if I do it all wrong? I don't want to embarrass her. It's not only the whole Mom-in-a-box thing that scares me, but the cremation. What if after she becomes ash, she can't talk to me?

Ash isn't a body. I want someone held responsible for killing my mother, for taking her away from me. Once burned, she will cease to exist; might never have existed. But I exist. And because I am, my mother was. I watched the gleam of life flicker and go out from her eyes. I held her hand until her fingers felt limp. I am the witness to her life and death.

"Get in, July! I've got the heater on high."

I climb in the car. Mrs Gresham, in a dark blue dress and black woolen jacket, looks exactly as I expect her to, even the black hair band and the plain silver stud earrings. The car is warm, but I'm shaking. I sink down into the low seat and hold my juddering hands in my lap. My kneecaps begin twitching up and down, and there's a tic in my right cheek. I'm falling apart. If I disintegrate I won't have to burn my mother.

I crack the window and suck in the air, willing myself not to be sick.

"July, I'm listening if you want to talk," Mrs Gresham says patting my knee. Her voice brings me into the present.

I take a tissue out of my blazer pocket and blow my nose. I will hold together, whoever I am, I will be solid. "Thanks for coming to fetch me. It's really nice of you."

"I'll do more; you just tell me what you need."

"You have a dress for me?" I look around but don't see any bags in the car.

"They're in the boot. You can try them on once we get to the church. The pastor says we can use her office. I popped in a selection of shoes. I didn't know your size." She looks down at my feet. "Six or seven?"

"Five and a half, same as Mom's, they just look bigger in these boots. I wanted Doc Martens and Mom let me buy them for my birthday. They were very expensive. She said buying them made two people happy; me and her."

"Black?" She sounds amused.

"They had to be so I could wear them at school. I don't mind. Actually, I like them."

"Your mom liked sparkling shoes. She liked shiny everything!" She smiles at the memory.

I see my mother's taste in glimmer every time I open the door of our flat—the flash of light from the silver and gold curtains, a glint from the copper lamps, the shimmer of the silver threads in the carpet.

"Yes! Did you notice she had silver laces in her white work shoes?" Did Mrs Gresham know my mother as a vibrant nurse or only as a shadow woman?

"No, but of course that's exactly what your mom would do!" She turns on the left indicator.

"Um, Mrs Gresham, do you believe in ghosts?" I'm scared to share, but who else can I ask? She takes the question seriously.

"I think the other side isn't as far away as some people think, if that's what you're asking,"

"So if you hear or see someone who's dead, it doesn't mean you're going cuckoo and heading straight nonstop towards Rooidakkies, does it?" I watch her reaction. She's as serene as ever.

"It means you're dealing with loss in your own way. Is there someone you trust you can talk to?"

I nod and look out the window at the familiar streets and high-rise flats of Sunnyside. My home turf. Plastic grocery bags flap like miniature ghosts in the branches of the old jacaranda trees, some have fallen and landed spread-out on the barbed wire fences. More bags roll like tumbleweed along the street. Beer bottles and plastic containers lie in the gutters. The air smells of rotting food and human shit. Battered minibuses race across red lights, risking annihilation to claim one more fare.

I look sideways at Mrs Gresham. "I trust you. I keep hearing my mother."

"What does she say?" She watches the road, not me. Somehow that makes it easier to speak.

"All the stuff she always told me about safety and how to do things, and who to think about, that kind of thing." It's such a release to talk about my worries.

"You feel she's still caring for you?"

"Yes. She's still around. For now."

"For now?"

If I expose my deepest fear will it become real? I don't want to activate the bad forces, but if I don't take this chance to talk I think I'll explode. I gather up all my willpower and whisper, "Will she still talk to me when she's ash?" Fear sinks its claws deeper into my heart; I lean forward clutching my chest in pain. Mrs Gresham pats my knee. It doesn't help.

"Your mother was a strong believer in the afterlife. She believed she'd still exist in a different form. Why would that form not be able to speak, especially to her beloved daughter?"

I sit back. The pain ebbs away. What do living people know about reality on the dead side? Anything is possible. Mrs Gresham's words ignite a tiny ember of hope in me.

In the pastor's office, Mrs Gresham shows me the clothes. "Let's get you changed. I found this black skirt that you can wear with your school shirt, or there's this black sheath dress, and a black wool jacket to keep you warm. Oh and this black beret, if you want to wear a hat, and black tights. I did find a pair of size five-and-half black shoes."

"I'll wear the dress." Picking it up, I look around for a private place to change. There is none.

"I'll look out the window," Mrs Gresham says noticing my hesitancy.

I take off my uniform and hear Mrs Gresham gasp. She's seen my burns, bruises, and cuts.

"Who did this to you?" She comes up to me, her face pale with shock.

"I don't know exactly." I step away sensing she wants to hug me. I turn around and pull on the dress, concentrating on doing up the zip and fastening the belt. If I think about the rape it might initiate the black feathers and I need to stay present for Mom's final public appearance.

"Did you go to the police?"

"Yes, the same night. They told me to go home."

I sit down and take off my boots and socks and pull on the tights. I want her to stop with the questions. Today is about Mom, not me.

"Have you seen a doctor? They have to take swabs and do tests."

"No. I went home and had a bath." I close my eyes and feel her take my hands. I open my eyes to find her kneeling in front of me. I pull back in surprise.

"You poor child, you don't have to go through this alone anymore. I'm here. I will help you. Let's honour your mother today, then you come and stay at my house and I'll care for you."

"Yes, I will; thank you. May I try on the shoes?"

She stands up and gets them. "They have kitten heels."

"And they fit me." I stand up and walk around.

"You look perfect. Let me do your hair. I bought you a new brush."

She brushes my hair and adds a wide hair band, then places the black woolen beret on my head. I examine myself in the mirror. Mirror girl appears calm, cared for, stylish, someone who will leave this place and go home to her mother, a cooked supper, and an evening in front of the television. She definitely knows how to do funerals. Her face is serious. I trust her.

Mrs Gresham glances at the clock on the wall. "Are you ready? We're meeting the pastor in the foyer. She'll go first and then we'll follow."

I let mirror girl lead the way. She will perform this act. I'll be the shadow.

17. THE FUNERAL

A RUSTLE FLOWS DOWN the pews towards me as people turn around to stare. Scrutinized, I smooth down the borrowed dress and pull at the jacket. Ahead of me the middle of the church appears hollow because everyone is wearing black. The place is packed. Someone reaches out to touch me. I back away. My skin crawls. Stop it! I want to scream, but there's a pebble lodged in my throat. I cough to move it but it doesn't budge.

Mrs Gresham takes my hand. "July, dear, we're going to walk down the aisle to the front, there's a spot reserved for us there." I hang on to her, one steady point in a confusing world. As I take my first step the organ begins to play and the crowd rises to its feet in another long rush of rustling and sniffling.

I recognize the song. "That's 'Hallelujah' by Kathy Troccoli. Mom loves it."

Mrs Gresham nods and keeps pulling me forwards.

Up above me, a large choir begins singing, and the congregation joins in full volume eager to contribute. I look up at the ceiling expecting the beams to sway with the force. The music unifies us; one sound, one people, one grief. Goosebumps break out across my skin. I'm submerged in a pool of harmony, fully enveloped yet still breathing; a fish in a bowl of sound, apart from the world of loss. Here I am safe.

The blue carpet before me is running out. I slow down. I don't want to do this. I want to run away. Mrs Gresham gently tugs my arm. I coax myself, you can do this, left foot, right foot, and again. Mind that handbag in the aisle, avoid the outstretched hand. Nearly there. We get to where we don't want to be. The coffin. My Mom.

It's a pine box balanced on a black metal stand. One large bunch of pink roses at the head and an equally large bunch of white roses at her feet.

I never thought of flowers. Sorry Mom.

The sweet scent veils my face as I sit down on the chair closest to the coffin. Mrs Gresham sits next to me and pushes her handbag under her chair. I don't have a bag. I can't breathe real air, only the scented stuff. I feel light-headed. I won't faint. This is for Mom. She says I'm strong and courageous. Today, I am, though it seems that being strong and courageous means doing things you don't want to do, things that bring you no pleasure or benefit.

I stare ahead at the plain wooden cross on the wall. Mom is close but not as I want her to be. She's in there. Should I look? No, it is closed. Mom didn't want it open. Is she really in there? How do I know? I have to trust Mrs Gresham.

"Hi Mom," I whisper touching the box. It's smooth and cold under my hand. I flatten my palm on to the wood. "Are you watching this, Mom? You have a lot of friends."

The music stops and Pastor Nkoli, a stocky woman with cropped brown hair, rises and asks everyone to shift along to create space for new arrivals. Although Mom liked her, worked with her at the same hospital and counted her as a close friend, she never brought her home. I don't know why and it's too late to ask.

The organ plays. It's another one of Mom's favourites, the Vineyard song "Hide Me in the Shelter." The words are displayed on the screen. Had Mom chosen the songs to send me special messages? Did this one say she'd made it to heaven? I wish I had a paper and a pen to write down the titles. Then I realize they are all listed in the handout Mrs Gresham gave me.

My fear and pain turn to resentment. Thirty-six is too young to die; she was murdered with an infected needle. Mom is dead and her killer alive and free. We couldn't afford any of the new medications coming out that promised to stall HIV. But she never complained, never blamed, got on with preparing for the inevitable. Her first priority, giving me a paid-off home and plenty of money.

Thank you, Mom, but I have something to sort out first.

"That man who raped you."

My heart jumps. The voice didn't come from the coffin but some place close to my right ear. I turn to check, stupidly hopeful, but she's not there, only Mrs Gresham.

"Love you, Mom!" It feels so good to say that. I know I'm smiling. It feels like I'm wrapped in a soft, heated blanket.

"Love you too, Darling."

"I know it's all a mess now. I have a plan to fix it."

"You are strong. I raised you to be able to see your vision and walk towards it. I know you will succeed. You're a good person. Be courageous."

"You made me feel strong."

"My darling, look up at that empty cross. Jesus achieved his mission. You were made by God to achieve yours. You have something special for the world. I know you'll achieve it."

"It's hard to be strong when you're alone."

"Look around you for the good people. You are not alone. Let them help you."

"Will you still speak to me when they cremate your body?"

"I'm not in my body, Honeybear."

The song ends. Everyone sits down. The pastor steps up to the wooden podium and speaks into the microphone.

"Ms Catherine Abraham, July's mother, was an active

member of this church, a busy nurse, and a willing hand to
all who asked of her. A generous person, she is already greatly
missed. I considered her a good friend. I valued her calmness,
her sincerity and her wit. I will now open the mike up to any
who would like to say a few words about her. Be specific in
what you say and say it quickly, then more people will get a
chance to share." She steps down and returns to her chair on
the other side of the coffin.

One by one people of all races come forward to speak
of Mom's generosity, sense of humour, and above all, her
compassion.

"People always remember kindness," Mrs Gresham whispers.

These strangers mean well but their words diffuse my loss.
She's my mom and this is my private loss. They don't go home
to no-Mom. What do they know about losing her? Why must
I share this with them? I glare at the current speaker and he
holds my gaze.

" . . . you need anything you let me know. I'll do it. The
pastor here has my number. You bell, I'll help." He makes the
thumb and finger phone and brings it to his ear. Is he my
father? Mom asked for a small funeral; no blurb in the papers,
no horde. It's all spun sideways. I'm at risk. I don't know what
Mr Stedman looks like, but he knows me. Is he watching me? I
want to be left alone. Mom and I have a plan, I want to live it.

The Pastor is at the microphone. She tells us all to sing. We
stand and the organ sounds out the notes of "He Knows My
Name" by Tommy Walker.

As the song ends, the Pastor says, "July—would you like to
come up to the mike and say a few words?"

I didn't expect this. No one warned me. I shake my head. I
can't talk: stone in my throat.

Mrs Gresham hands me a tissue and rubs my arm. "Go up and just try. You will find the strength to talk about your mom."

The pastor lowers to mike to my level then returns to her chair.

Seeing all the sad faces exposed in their grief turns my legs to water. If I fall over right here they won't force me to speak will they? Then I remember, this is all for Mom, not me. I clear my throat and the sound, magnified by the PA system, bounces off the walls and comes back to me as if belonging to someone else. Now I feel relaxed enough to speak.

"Mom, my mother, was great. We only had each other. I put up with her two-hour candle-lit soaks in the bath, and we both liked watching British TV shows and eating Marmite toast and savory scrambled eggs. I miss all the small things. It's a constant stream of missing. She used to sing when she cooked: Neil Diamond and John Denver. 'Some days are Diamond' got a lot of air time. As she got sicker, I couldn't carry her, I had no choice but to call Mrs Gresham's hospice, as planned. I didn't want to but, you know, it is what it is. Mom planned every-thing so well. Now I'm unplanned and without her . . . " I lift my hands to show my helplessness. I notice people nodding, others wipe their eyes. I've said enough.

I kiss my hand and place it on the lid of the coffin. "Love you, Mom."

Returning to my seat, I notice a very familiar face at the back of the church. I miss the chair and land on the floor. Mrs Gresham rushes to help me up. I peer down the aisle to see if who I thought I saw is still there. No. Am I hallucinating?

The organ plays the introductory notes to "He will come and save you" by Gary Sadler. The congregation stands up to sing. I'm shaking from my ankles to my ears. School and Mom can't exist together. That is not the plan. Like a tornado ripping apart a home, my whole world is disintegrating.

Six men come forward, lift the coffin, and begin walking down the aisle. Mrs Gresham takes my arm and guides me out.

Cool air hits me as the double doors open to the outside, and we pause to watch the back of the minivan lift up and the coffin placed inside.

"Come, July, we'll get my car and follow behind."

My head is empty. Not a word, not a thought, not a feeling. Mrs Gresham takes my hand and I realize that I don't need my brain. I am not required to think or plan anything.

18. FINAL LETTER

MRS GRESHAM UNLOCKS HER front door and ushers me inside. "Here we are. In you go." She switches on the hall light, then locks up and drops her keys into her handbag.

The place is tiny: a four-step box with three doors to my left. Mrs Gresham goes on to the farther end. Here are a wooden counter with a small fridge underneath, wall shelves, a sink, and a gas stove. On the opposite wall a love seat and an armchair surround a gas heater. In the centre are a circular table with two chairs.

"Come sit down at the table. I'll put the kettle on for tea."

I sit at the table, in front of a pink bowl and metal spoon.

Mrs Gresham closes the curtains and clicks the gas heater to life; it hisses and splutters before its square heart glows orange.

"The benefits of a small space; it warms in no time and uses very little gas. Here let me help you with that jacket." She takes my jacket and beret and drops them on the love seat.

"Supper's ready. I had someone switch the oven on for me so it would be ready around now." Taking oven gloves from a hook on the wall, she removes a casserole dish of bubbling lasagna and places it on the table.

"Careful, it's very hot." She serves me one spoonful and herself two.

I'm a shadow and shadows don't eat; they don't feel, they don't hurt.

"Shall I take your bowl?" Mrs Gresham asks standing up from the table.

I nod. I haven't taken a bite. She doesn't comment.

"I'll make some hot chocolate. I've put a hot water bottle in your bed and switched on the little bar heater in the room. You'll be nice and snug."

My eyes stray over to the kitchen counter. On it is the silver and gold urn containing Mom's ashes. Her last residence? No, she's not in there. She exists unrestricted by earth's physical or social laws. Gravity does not pull her down, borders do not push her out, and no body confines her. She is free. I envy her.

Pain shoots up my neck and into my head. I clutch my hair and massage my scalp. Is this what dying feels like? Wait up Mom, I'm coming. I image her running to greet me, arms wide ready for a hug. I lean forward eager to feel her warmth.

The microwave pings and Mrs Gresham removes the mugs of hot chocolate. She must have seen me studying the urn because she says, "I can keep the urn here if you want me to, until you make your decision."

"What decision?" I ask. Her ashes are the very last bits I'll ever have of Mom; I want them with me for always.

"Well, when your mother's Will is read, we'll find out if she has any directives as to what she wants done with her ashes. I'm hoping the lawyers won't take too long. I'll phone you when I hear from them."

"I will keep them. It's not a problem."

"Good," she says. "Tomorrow, I'd like you to sleep in, take things slow, no school. Then I'll take you to Brooklyn Centre for waffles. What do you think?"

"Someone from my school was at the church. Now my school will know. They'll phone the authorities. I'll be put in care. Mom doesn't want me in care. We have a plan. Has it failed already? What do I do?"

"Is the person a friend of yours?" She sits back in her chair and watches me. I absorb some of her calmness.

"A new friend."

"Are they trustworthy?"

"I think so. I don't know really. What if they've already shared it? Such a big funeral doesn't look very secretive."

"Well why not ask them to keep your secret? Would they listen?"

"Maybe. They seem responsible. But if they're not, then what? Mom made all the plans."

Mrs Gresham pats my hand. "I'm here to help you. Don't worry. We'll get through it."

"I turn sixteen next year. Then Welfare can't touch me. I can live alone."

One whole year is a long time to keep such a huge secret. Was it even possible? Maybe we made a mistake not having a plan B. Where does that leave me? How do I prepare for consequences we never considered, like foster homes, an orphanage, a father?

"You are not alone. I'm here."

She is sincere but wrong, I am alone because no one else will ever place me first in their lives, like Mom did. Now I compete for attention in other people's lives.

A car drives past on the street outside, its music blaring on all speakers. The doom, doom, doom of the bass lasts long after the noise of the engine has drained away. Lives have after-beats too, I think, vibrations that linger, actions that change the world of the living forever.

"I have something your Mom asked me to give you today." Mrs Gresham says and reaches into her pocket and places a white envelope on the table. The envelope says:

To July My Darling Daughter

Seeing Mom's large curvy handwriting brings her into the room. I run my fingers softly over the letters. These are real solid words from her. Words I can see, touch, and keep, not like the ones I hear her speak that fade away.

Mrs Gresham gets up. "I'll go and run your bath and leave you to read in peace. I'll put in some Radox salts." She leaves me to my letter.

I remove the single sheet, hungry for contact.

July, my darling, precious, wonderful daughter. This has been a difficult day for you. I love you with my whole heart, never forget that. I know that you are strong, able, and courageous and can do anything you want. You are smart, and careful with it. You are determined and hard-working: a combination that gives success. I know you will be a very powerful and successful woman.

Please take things slowly. Grieve. Be gentle with yourself. Let Mrs Gresham take care of you. Buy those tubs of vanilla yoghurt you love. Make yourself your favourite strawberry banana smoothies. Get to bed early. Get lots of rest. I have told Mrs Gresham you like lasagna and shepherd's pie, so expect to be fed them. I gave her my recipes to use just for you. I find hot baths relieve stress. You can use my bath salts—even the citrus ones.

About family, I never married your father because I didn't want a husband. Your father knows about you. I sent him photographs of you over the years, but we never got together. He isn't married. He knows it is your choice to meet him. Here are his details again. Honeybear, your father exists on earth right now and I need to know that there is someone there for you. I believe he is a good man. Julius Stedman 082 808 5666

My strong beautiful child, I'll love you forever, and I'll always be your Mommy.

XOXOXOXOXOXOXOXOXOXOXOXOXOXOXOXOXO
XOXOXOXOXOXOXOXOXOXO

I want to claim each one of those kisses and hugs right now. My eyes are leaking, they will ruin the letter. I put it back in the envelope. I need a tissue and put my hand into my pocket. I have no pockets. This isn't my dress. Exhausted and unsure of what to do, I sit and let the tears drop on the table.

"July, your bath's ready," Mrs Gresham says coming into the room. "I've switched on the bathroom heater. There are fresh towels. If I've forgotten anything, tell me. I know I'll have it."

Picking up the envelope, I look up at Mrs Gresham. "Yes. Thank you. Thank you."

Mrs Gresham takes a tissue out of the box on a kitchen shelf and hands it to me. "And you can stay here with me for as long as you need."

"I'd like that, thank you. I must go to school tomorrow."

I can see she is surprised.

"Okay, then I'll drive you there and collect you." She opens a drawer and places keys on the table. "Here are the keys to the front door and the security gate, and here is my mobile number. I have yours. You can reach me any time, and I mean 24/7."

"Thank you." I give her a hug. "Also there's a party tomorrow night that is important. I've planned to go to it for some time. I won't get the chance again."

She's shocked and sits down opposite me. "Because I care, I have to ask: where and with whom?"

"A plot in Mnandi. I'll let you know as soon as I have the exact details."

"Will you be safe?" I can see her recalling the state of my body.

"Yes, nobody will hurt me again."

"Do you want to talk about it?" She looks me in the eye, assessing my stability.

"Not tonight. Thanks, don't worry, I'll be fine. Goodnight." I get up and walk to the door.

"Well, all I can say is, it's a good thing I trust you. I put two

Panados and a glass of water ncxt to your bed. Take them and get some sleep. If you change your mind and decide to stay home tomorrow I'll be very relieved."

"Thank you. 'Night." I walk away sagging under the weight of the day. Too many faces, expectations, orders, and endings. Tonight I cease to be. July Part One ends. Tomorrow I wake up into my new existence and a world I will improve for myself and all girls.

19. FRIDAY SCHOOL

"UNIFORM INSPECTION! GET READY for uniform inspection!" The prefects call as we wait in the hall after Friday morning assembly. I watch everyone start checking themselves and their friends for infractions. It's like we're monkeys searching for fleas and lice before the head monkey sentences us to a delousing dip. It's serious business; nobody wants to delay their weekend sitting in detention for having the wrong colour socks. I can't pass this check and the consequences suit me; detention is a safe zone. The boys file out through the door to the left into south quad, and we file through the door on the right into north quad.

Hemmed in between Khetiwe and Lily, I shuffle forward with the grade tens, questioning my choice of this over a lazy morning in bed followed by waffles at the mall. School is pointless, totally unrelated to the real world. Who cares if you have painted nails? The world keeps revolving.

Our prefect's name is Letsha. She snaps at me, "Nails, make-up? Take off that jacket, it's not school blue. You have a blazer."

"No, I need it. I'm really cold." I'm shaking. She can see it.

She barks, "Why not wear a blue jersey under your blazer, and thick stockings and socks under your trousers, everyone else does. Take off that green parka. We have rules. Hand it over, I'm confiscating it for a week." She holds out her hand. I shake my head. She glares at me and takes out her Detention book.

"Please Letsha, don't! July is allowed her coat," Lily steps forward. "Ms Botha knows about it."

That's a fat lie! I stare at Lily in wonder. Is she defending me because she saw me at the church? It proves she was really there.

"Then give me the Permission Slip," Letsha says putting her open palm under my nose.

"She doesn't have it right now," Lily says. "I can bring it to you later."

"Bring it to me in the prefects' room at first break."

Lily nods and leads me away. Letsha starts on Khetiwe.

Outside the hall, I free myself from Lily's hand. "Thanks. How will you get a slip from Ms Botha?" I ask, staring at her, waiting for her to own up to seeing me at the church.

Lily's blue eyes fill with tears. She searches in her pocket for her tissue bag and removes one to wipe her eyes. "I will. I want to help in any way I can."

I pull her into a quiet corner of the cloister. "It was you. I saw you. Why were you there?"

"My mom's church was SOS-called to help with the catering; more people than expected. I went with her. Why didn't you tell us your mom was sick?"

"If the school finds out, they will report me to Welfare. I'll be taken into care. I don't want that. I have a place to live and money."

Lily nods. "I understand. I wouldn't want that either."

"Did you see anyone else from this part of town at the church?"

"No." She wipes her eyes. "What can I do to help you?"

"Did you tell anyone about it?"

"No. I did wonder why you hadn't told us. I knew it had to be a secret."

"Yes. It has to be a secret until I turn sixteen. You can't even tell Khetiwe. Please."

She nods. "Sure. I understand."

Khetiwe arrives and the three of us set off for our registration classroom where Lily fails to extract a Permission Slip out of Ms Botha. Instead, Lily convinces me to take off my jacket, put on her spare school jersey, and let her put my offending garment in my locker. She's mothering me and I appreciate it.

As I walk from class to class I feel like life took its biggest rucksack, stuffed my previous existence inside, and dropped it on my shoulders, saying, "You don't get to live this any more but you will carry it forever." Just putting one leg in front of the other requires all my concentration and effort. I stagger like I've run the Comrade's marathon; the harder one from Durban to Pietermaritzburg. Maybe Mrs Gresham knew about this after-death rubber leg occurrence and recommended I spend the day resting. If I can't even walk now, where will I find the strength to take down the rapist tonight?

As if reading my thoughts, Lily says,

"I think we should cancel tonight. There'll be other parties."

"You and Khetiwe don't need to go. I'm still going." I regret involving Lily and Khetiwe. They're safer out of it.

"Oh, no, no, I didn't mean we don't want to come with you," Lily says. "You're doing this for us and we will be there to help you. Unity is strength after all. Hey, why don't we meet up at my house today after school? My mom will fetch us in the car if I ask her. Then we can, you know, plan everything and catch a ride to the party with Darren. And you are welcome to sleep over. We have enough beds and my mom loves looking after people."

"Yes, definitely. I'll call my mom right now." Khetiwe takes out her phone.

"I'm in," I say, pleased to leave all the planning to Lily. I phone Mrs Gresham. She asks for Lily's mother's number but is otherwise okay with the arrangement.

Lily says, "July, we can drop by your place to pick up anything you need."

"I've got it all in my locker. I spent last night at a friend's." Her question triggers the knowledge that I hid my tracksuit in a drawer of the sickroom, I have to move it to my locker.

Before she pushes open the classroom door, Lily gives my arm a squeeze, "I really am very sorry about your mom," she whispers. "I'll do anything I can to help."

I accept the squeeze. After this lesson, I'll go up to the sick room and get my tracksuit.

20. NOTICED

> We know where you sleep

A SMALL WHITE BUSINESS card is stapled to the collar of my track top when I take it out of the sickroom drawer. It feels like the full load of a logging truck lands on me. Pinned under the weight, blinded by fear, only the thud of my heart-beat proves I'm still alive. I must get out of this room, but is it safe to open the door and leave? Are they already outside?

I look at the tiny space between the base of the door and the floor. There is no shadow interrupting that narrow strip of sunlight. If they have followed me up here, they are not standing close enough for me to see them. I lie flat on the floor and look under the door. I see sunlight on empty tiles.

Do I stay or leave? Dare I open the door? How did Richter find out I've slept here? Who told him? The hairs on my arms are on end. A shudder travels through my body, my jaw vibrates. I don't want to die, get put in a box, and shoved into the fire. I have to escape. The black feathers invade my eyes, erasing my vision. Helpless, I sit on the bed and let the waves of fear and misery crash over me, knowing that like all waves they will spend their energy and ebb away.

Mom is in the kitchen listening to Radio 702. She's chopping carrots, peeling potatoes and plopping them into a pot. It's an ordinary evening. The front door is locked and the curtains drawn. The stew

bubbles on the stove, filling the air with a beefy fragrance. Mom dances
to a pop tune: "Walking on Sunshine." I laugh and get up to join
her . . .

As I watch the door of the sickroom, the last wave dribbles
slowly back to the sea. I stand up and walk towards the door,
determined to get away.

Knock, knock . . . knock.

Clearly I can't die from shock, because if I could I'd be
sprawled out on the grey linoleum, exuding body gases. I reach
in my pocket for my knife while staring down the shadow under
the door. Who could it be? Not a teacher and not Richter. I
can't find my knife. I dig frantically into all three pockets of my
blazer then realize my knife is in my jacket now hanging in my
locker. I look around for some kind of weapon and grab the
pillowcase off the pillow. I can pull it over his head and give
myself time to run. I watch the door, mouth dry, heart pounding.

The handle turns and the door opens. Blonde hair, blue eyes
all set in a handsome face look at me.

"Hey—it's you," Peter McNeil says, stepping inside and
looking around. "Just you?" He looks at me suspiciously from
my boots to my head. "How did you get in here? Where's Mrs
Prince?"

"She's under the bed," I reply, putting down the pillowcase
and going towards the door to leave.

He closes the door and leans against it, hands in pockets, like
he's settling in for a long stay. My stomach lurches as my brain
hands me the situation update: Peter McNeil is not benign. I
reach for the pillowcase.

"What are you doing in here?" He's all law-and-order; confident in his rightness.

"Mrs Prince said I should lie down. I have a headache." He's
much taller than me. How would I get the pillowcase over his
head?

"And there's just you up here?" He scans the room again. A flame of anger burns in me, I'm tired of being threatened. I glare at him.

"No, it's a full-on rave of four thousand screaming lunatics. Open your eyes. Now get out of my way. I'm leaving." I take the two steps to the door. He doesn't flinch. He doesn't move. He smiles.

We are so close I can smell him, that pleasant mixture of incense and fresh laundry. I can't trust him. I'm alone here, and without my knife I can't defend myself. Then I remember the keys in my pocket. If I place each one between my fingers, I'll have a makeshift knuckle duster to slice through his grin.

"Listen, there's something I want to ask you," he says, shifting his back into a comfier spot.

"Get out my way or I'll scream." I take half a step closer. I know how the game of chicken works.

He raises his hand. "Just hang on. Okay. Listen up. I followed Travis Richter up here. He saw me and ran down. I decided to come up and see what was going on, and found you. Which, you have to admit, seems to beg the question: why? What are you two up to?"

"There is no *two* when it comes to Richter and me." He's standing near enough that I can administer a swift kick to his nuts that will put him out of commission. My jaw is going numb and my arms tingle with pins and needles.

"He's not a guy who pays attention to people who are not useful to him, which means you must be; which means you need help. I can get that for you. Trust me. I can get you help."

That gentle voice, charming and seeming to care, so seductive, offering kindness. I feel its pull, I do need help. Then the words to a nursery rhyme arrive: "Come into my parlour said the spider to the fly" and I wake up to the danger.

"Read my lips," I say. "I'm not involved in any way with

Travis Richter. Okay? Now get out of my way or I will scream." My words emerge slurred because my face is frozen like after a dentist's visit. He sighs and his tone reflects his belief that my IQ is negative four hundred.

"I really am trying to help you. If not now, then think of it as an open offer."

I try to say, "I want to go downstairs. I'm not feeling well," but my eyes are leaking what feels like battery acid and the pins and needles have taken over my legs. I fall.

I'm in his lap. I can see his grey trouser pants stretched over his knees. His shoes are very shiny and his socks regulation blue. His belt buckle is pressed against my cheek. I must escape. I am not safe.

I push away screaming, "Get away. Get away from me! Let me out of here! Help! Help! Somebody help me!" I hit him and kick him. He dumps me on the floor and scrambles out of reach.

"Okay, okay, stop yelling. I'll go and fetch someone. Will you be okay alone here?"

I blink and look around. Tears drip off my chin and down my shirt. Peter stands at the open door, his eyes wide, face white, body tense for action. Sunlight streams across the top stair. My nightmare passes, but Richter is still out there.

"No! Don't leave me alone here."

He takes a deep breath and steps closer. "What do you want me to do? I'll carry you down to the office if you want."

"Yes. Take me to Mrs Prince."

With great care, he scoops me up like an oversized baby and carries me down to the office.

Depositing me on the chair in Mrs Prince's cubicle, he tells her, "Excuse me, Mrs Prince. July is really sick. She needs help." He holds my shoulder making sure I don't keel over.

"Not again, July. You poor thing. Shame. Thank you, Peter,

you've been very helpful. I'll take it from here."

After one last shoulder squeeze, he leaves.

Mrs Prince feels my forehead. "Oh my, love, you don't look at all well." She places a box of tissues on my lap, taking one out to wipe my wet face and snot nose. I'm waiting for her to play Mom and say, "Blow." Luckily, she doesn't.

"It's my head. It's really pounding." I push my fingers into the exact spot above my ears. "That rabbit is still trying to kick its way free." The box of tissues slips from my lap on to the floor. I don't have the energy to pick it up.

"This is happening a lot. I think it's time to call your mother to come and fetch you. You need to see a doctor." She reaches for her phone.

"My mother can't get here," I tell her, to stop the inevitable. The office is a safe space. I want to stay here a while. "Those Panados you gave me last time worked well."

"I'll get them, but I'm still going to call your mom, she must come and collect you. You look terrible."

I shake my head. "No, I'll be fine. I can't miss Afrikaans." I prepare to stand up, hoping my body will cooperate. "Do I get a late note from you?"

"You wait right there. Don't move. I'll get you the pills for now, but you must go and see a doctor." She leaves. I close my eyes. I can't fall apart now; tomorrow, yes, today, no.

"Here." Mrs Prince presses the tablets into my hand with a small cup of water. "I've put the kettle on. I didn't get hold of your mother. The sickroom is free. I'll bring you a cup of tea and then take you up there."

"No. I don't want to go there. I'll be fine after a cup of tea. Thank you."

I'm tired and dizzy. I want to go home and sleep, jettison the mission, try again another time when I'm stronger. But I know that if I don't take care of the rapist tonight he might strike again. I won't let that happen. I sip the tea Mrs Prince brings and eat the egg sandwich I think she took from her own lunch box. Placing the empty cup under my chair, I settle back and fall asleep.

The bell ringing wakes me.

Mrs Prince says, "Good morning. Do you want to go to class or go home? It's the last lesson of the day."

I sit up and look at my watch. "I'll go back. Thank you."

The nap has helped. I feel stronger. Walking across the quad to maths, I decide to stay safe by keeping close to Lily and Khetiwe.

Kevin appears around a corner and walks past me saying, "Don't go tonight. They are waiting for you. I'm not going." He pushes open the classroom door, I follow him in.

His words don't change a thing; tonight belongs to me.

21. LILY'S HOUSE

A MISTAKE, A BAD MISTAKE. When I blacked out in the sickroom a software bug must have invaded my brain making it forget to do the constant safety checks and updates I need to stay alive. Now I'm in danger.

In agreeing to spend the night at Lily's house and go to the party with her and her brothers, I forgot that Darren Wesley is a good friend of Lucas du Toit. Lucas du Toit is the man I think is the rapist, and he now knows exactly where I will be spending my next hours. He doesn't have to hunt me down; I'm delivering myself to him. It's the small mistakes that take a person down. I'm like a race horse stumbling out of the starting gate and breaking its leg even before the race gets going.

Lily sits in the front. Her mother, an older faded Lily with a tight blond bun, drives. Khetiwe sitting next to me in the back smiles when I look at her. I nod and smile. We speed up the steep Lukasrand Hill. The road is another tunnel of high walls. Swinging a hairpin right and a quick left we arrive at a set of tall security gates with a camera perched on top. As the gates clang closed behind us I'm paralyzed with panic; trapped. The long, stone bungalow with solar panels on the roof looks solid like a fortress. If I run from the car as soon as it stops, I'll look crazy. Looking crazy is better than being dead. I can't open the door—am I that weak?

"Child locks," Lily's mother says noticing my fumbling.

Lily is my age, why do they still have child locks on the doors? My mind jumps to a bundle of deceit, and in it lies Lily, her mother, and Darren. No! I trust Lily. My life hangs on that one thin thread; let it be catgut.

We drive up to one of the four garages chiseled out of the rock under the home.

At school Lily filled us in on her family's garage-door drill. It all started five weeks previous when Andrew, the neighbour's tall, red-headed, rugby playing son, returned home from school to find armed men inside the garage. They shot him dead. He was eighteen years and five days old. That night Lily's dad installed the latest detection devices inside and outside the garages; no one can move around any part of this property and house without activating an alarm.

As the garage door begins to open, Mrs Wesley crouches down in her seat and we do the same so that if bullets are fired the car's shell will protect us.

The garage door closes and a circular light on the wall turns green. I hear a set of pips, and Mrs Wesley says, "We're clear to leave. Lily, please let your friends out."

I'm out the car but not free.

Carrying our bags, we clatter up iron stairs to a steel door. Mrs Wesley swipes her finger over a small black box and the door clicks open to reveal a corridor. We move inside and the door automatically closes behind us. Lily failed to mention the finger-swipe machine. Khetiwe doesn't comment either. They must use them all the time. My flat's front door has a security gate and extra bolts. I use a key to get into the building. If tonight's party house in Mnandi has this type of security I won't be able to move around undetected. I'll have to blend in with the crowd, people I don't know who, according to Kevin, will be watching for me. Will my lumbering brain keep me alert to this fact? Assuming I leave this house in one piece.

Through another door we step into a light airy entrance foyer. There is a coat rack and a long side table hosting a huge

bowl of sweet-smelling red roses. Off to my left is the imposing
double front door—finally a simple escape route even with its
security camera and flashing red lights.

We swipe dance our way into a large kitchen: shiny granite
surfaces, stainless steel appliances, gleaming white double sink,
and nothing on any counter except another bowl of flowers.
Where is their real kitchen, the one with the kettle, cook,
housemaid, and a pot of food on the stove? I stand with my
back against the fridge. No one can jump me from behind.

"I planned baked beans on toast?" Mrs Wesley says locking
her handbag in a drawer and pocketing the key. Behind her
back, Khetiwe pulls a face at Lily and mimes an explosion with
her hands.

"Can we switch the baked beans for spaghetti rings?" Lily
asks, grinning.

"Consider it done," Mrs Wesley says. "What was I thinking?
Girls don't want gassy food before a party. Take Khetiwe and
July to their room, Lily. I've put them across from you. I'll buzz
you when the food is ready."

We follow Lily as she finger-swipes open a wide door to the
right. We enter a formal sitting room. The grey marble floor
is covered in a red oriental carpet. It looks like a room I've
seen in the *Architectural Digest* magazines at school. Perfectly
positioned lamps, paintings, rugs, and knick-knacks displayed
to show style and wealth. It smells faintly of Pledge furniture
polish. It is the smell of Mom's cleaning. She loved Pledge.
She'd even spray it into the air when we didn't have time to
clean, calling it a cheat-clean. My heart twists; it's a physical
pinch, sharp and lingering, prodding an invisible and incurable
wound.

From the sitting room, Lily opens a door into a wide
corridor. Here the art work is all family photographs of chris-
tenings, weddings, and vacations.

"Are any of your brothers home yet?" Khetiwe asks. I tune in, anxious to hear the answer.

"No. Darren will be back around five and Grant is at school playing squash. Last time I heard, they've both decided to come with us." We walk past three doors. The passage curves to the right.

"Is Darren bringing any friends with him?" I ask, metronoming between trust and danger.

"Yes, Erin King," Lily says. "He's stoked about her. It's the first time she's agreed to go on a date with him." She stops outside a door on the left. "This is my room."

I take a deep breath, preparing for a hood over my head, or a knock-out needle, and follow them into a huge room. Light floods in through its tall windows. There's a four-poster bed, a fireplace, a desk, several bookshelves, and a wall of wardrobes. I eye them suspiciously. Please don't let Lucas or Richter jump out of them.

Khetiwe, obviously familiar with the room, opens a cupboard and starts going through the clothes.

I trace out an engraving of a bunch of grapes on one of the bed posts. "I've never seen a real four-poster. How did you get it in here? Is it really old?"

Lily drops her school bag on her desk and walks over. "It was made for my great grandmother as a wedding gift from her parents, made right here in this house, just before the Second Boer War. The wood is teak and hard as nails. When my folks got a new one made, they had this one dismantled, moved into my room and reassembled. It's a family heirloom."

"It's lovely." I move across to the windows and note their narrow-spaced bars; no escape here. "You can see the Union Buildings from here, and all the way across Sunnyside to Hatfield Plaza. I'd put my desk right here at the window."

"Too hot; it faces north." Lily pushes aside the net curtains.

"When the jacarandas are in bloom the whole valley is covered in purple, like low-lying purple clouds. It makes me think of Prince's song 'Purple Rain'."

"You listen to Prince? I had you down for Carike Keuzenkamp and Steve Hofmeyr."

She shoots me an indignant look.

"I'm fifteen, July, I listen to what I want, and I know Prince's 'Purple Rain' is old, but I like it." She flounces over to her bed and throws a small pillow at me.

I catch it and grin. "Hey, no criticism, I've heard 'When Doves Cry' from my baby days. My mom has his Purple Rain album."

She laughs. "So who do you listen to, Dozi?"

"Ladysmith Black Mambazo?" Khetiwe chimes in, laughing.

"At the moment I like Mango Groove and Savuka."

"Not bad. At least you didn't say P J Powers or éVoid." Lily gives me a wicked smile. "Have you heard of a guy called Rodriguez? He sings a song called 'Sugar Man'. It's got a good sound; laid back."

"Oh. Your father doesn't know what you're listening to. You stay away from songs about sugar." And I'm back buying marijuana for my mom and trusting Andre Vermarck. "Just stay away from all drugs." I see her eyebrows rise, and she looks across at Khetiwe.

Khetiwe gives a tiny nod.

I brace myself for something unpleasant. Is this when they spring the trap? I feel in my pocket for my knife.

22. TRUST

"JULY, CAN I ASK A QUESTION?" Khetiwe asks, choosing a red, flowing blouse from the cupboard and draping it over her knee as she sits down. She's watching me. Lily settles on the bed. I stay at the window, at the apex of a triangle of discomfort.

"Sure. Go ahead," I say, with an eye on the cupboards and the door for a sudden influx of people.

"Do you deal or take drugs? Everyone at school says you do."

It feels like a learned script, a planned intervention.

"No, I have never taken or sold drugs. I did buy marijuana for my mother. She was very sick and had a lot of pain. It helped her sleep."

"Your mother takes street drugs," Khetiwe says, her face puckering as if she's sucking on a lemon.

"She used to."

Another furtive look passes between my interrogators.

"How did you get the drugs?" Khetiwe asks.

"Well, being a first-time buyer I went to the person known for selling in our school, Andre Vermarck. He looks clean and acts polite."

Lily says, "So you're friends with Mpho Kageso. He's been stalking us at school. He's a friend of Andre Vermarck. I mean, you could be sucking us into this just to spit us out at the rapist's feet."

I almost laugh, hearing my own fear coming out of Lily's mouth. "No. I'm not. Andre is a dealer. He works for Travis Richter. You know him? Grade twelve, tall, thin, slicked back hair, shiny black jazz shoes, tight trousers; walks like someone shoved a carrot up his bum, drives a black BMW? Dealers are not friends. They are like great white sharks, one scent of blood and they attack. They supply their boss with girls. He's the rapist. I don't want anyone to end up there. Dealers are dangerous."

"But they know you and you know them," Khetiwe says, as if that's the definition of friendship. "And you haven't been raped. So you must be one of them."

My thoughts split into two. The first group says: show your wounds, prove yourself a victim. The second one cautions. As a victim I'll be judged as bitter and revengeful; labels slapped on all those who are denied justice. They might even see me as broken and defective. The sad, mad, bad labels used to denigrate and silence women. I won't wear a label, not even to prove a point.

"Richter and his gang are not my friends. They do not like me. They are dangerous. We are here to find the rapist and stop him hurting girls like you and me."

"You really don't know the rapist?" Lily asks placing a throw pillow on her lap.

"No." I lean back against the window, trying to look comfortable and relaxed. "It sounds like you don't trust me. If you want to back out now, I won't mind. We all need to put our own safety first. There's a bus stop at the bottom of the hill, I can get home easily." This could be my free ticket out of here.

Khetiwe says. "I know we've been in the same class for three years but, well, we don't really know you. And you do say some extreme things like cutting off the guy's balls and crushing his kneecaps. I mean if you do that we could all go to prison."

"What will you do if you are attacked? What if they take your knives off you? Do you know any self defense?" I ask. Lily pales and Khetiwe turns pink. I've increased their scare quotient to stratospheric levels. Good, it's time they woke up to the risks.

"Not tonight, this is a trial run," Lily says. "We'll stay close to my brothers and do some reconnaissance; identify the rapist and hand his name to the police. I don't want to attack anyone or upset them enough to attack me. That is not our plan."

"We only asked you to find him for us," Khetiwe says, examining her nails.

I sigh and stand up. Noticing that my moving sets them on edge, I sit back down and keep my expression serious. "We have a problem. It must be fixed."

Khetiwe strokes the red blouse on her knee like it's a cat. Lily hugs a pillow.

I plunge in. "How do I put this? It's a question of perception; your perception. I'm not sure you know how much danger you are in. At school you've seen Richter's boys watching us. They're doing it because you're friends of Andie. She's one of their victims who got away and can talk. They think she's spoken to you. Snitches threaten their boss's power. When you approached me, someone they know and hate, they figured you were passing on valuable information from Andie. They need you silenced. You can't see it, but you are both already on the battlefield. The enemy has you in their sights. If you won't fight, you at least have to defend yourselves."

"I don't want to go anymore," Khetiwe says. "It's a bad idea. We could get hurt." She tosses the blouse on to the bed.

"Yes! Exactly! I explained that back when you asked me to find the rapist for you."

"She's right. She did," Lily admits.

I dare to move from the window ledge down into the chair at Lily's desk. "To be up front, I don't know you two that well either. Trust works both ways. What if I end up hanging on to a rope that one of you is holding?" They look away from me;

not a good sign.

We are three. A triangle is a strong shape, but not a comfortable one. I look at my watch wondering how much time I have to catch that bus out of here.

The room has fallen silent. The clock on the bedside table clicks: stop, go, stop, go, stop . . .

"I'm still in," Lily announces. "I trust July. We have to get rid of this man and get our lives back."

Khetiwe's mouth drops open in disbelief. "But—no! Why? That's nuts!"

"Sometimes you have to be nuts to make things right," Lily says. "We'll stick together. You can do it."

Khetiwe gives Lily a look that should have stripped off her skin and nailed it to the wall.

"Really? We're going to do this even when we know better?" She shakes her head to show she doesn't agree with what she's about to say. "Fine, I'm in, but you two better stay with me all the time. And if anything goes wrong . . . "

"Then we'll face it together," I say. "Is that it? Is it final? We're doing it, as a team?"

We've all changed in each other's eyes. I'm more exotic, like Ebola; Lily's poodle has transformed into a lioness; and Khetiwe's caracal has its tail between its legs and wants to go home.

"Yes," they reply together and laugh at the coincidence.

Lily gets up and walks to the door. "Come, you two, your room is across the hall. Oh and remember the hallway cameras also pick up sound."

It's an en suite room with two double beds, a fireplace, a sofa and a love seat. I've never stayed in anything this fancy. I place my bag on the floor next to one of the beds and look out the window at an enclosed courtyard with a bench, trellised roses, a water feature, and no way to escape. I'm living on trust.

"I call dibs on the bed by the bathroom," Khetiwe says putting her bag on it.

"Come sit," Lily beckons, choosing the love seat. "What do we do first?" From her pocket she takes out a pen and paper.

Khetiwe sits next to Lily. "Yes, July, give us the plan that will save us."

I shake my head. "I don't have one. I've got a list of things to keep an eye on."

The intercom buzzes.

"Girls! Lunch is ready in the kitchen. You don't want it cold."

Lily runs to a grey box on the wall next to the door and presses a button.

"We're on our way, Mom." She turns around. "Last meal. Let's make it cheerful. No need to get anyone suspicious—especially my mother."

23. PARTY PLANNING

BACK IN OUR ROOM the fire's lit and the curtains have been drawn, proof that the invisible servants exist. I never imagined planning a manhunt in such a cozy corner. Lily and Khetiwe settle onto the love seat, pens and paper ready, faces tense, shoulders a little high. They are as scared as me, which is good because they'll be careful, but I think their ideal outcome and mine differ. Not that they need to know that. I want the result that keeps them, every girl, and me, safe from now on. Sitting on the sofa opposite them, I take my list from my blazer pocket.

"These are my ideas of how to stay safe tonight. We've already discussed the second one: keeping track of every boy in Richter's gang. We don't want them creeping up on us."

"I can't get my mind around why boys want to hurt girls," Khetiwe says. "It changes my ideas about going out with them. No one-on-one dates for sure. How do you know if a guy is good or bad?"

"Be prepared for the worst. If you can defend yourself, you stand a chance. My mom and I did self-defence training."

"But why do they do it?" Khetiwe is fixed on this one question.

"The short answer is: because they can. My mom says the expression 'Boys will be boys' gives boys a 'get out of jail free' card. They hear it since birth. They know they won't be punished for bad behaviour that hurts others; they know rules don't apply to them."

"That's why you keep on telling us to be able to defend ourselves," Khetiwe says, thoughtfully. "We're in a battle and we don't even know it. Now I understand why my mother made us move to Waterkloof—for our safety. She didn't explain in detail. She tries to protect me from the real world."

"We are at war. We're dying, being injured, taken prisoner, and sold into slavery. It's time girls realize this, form armies and fight back. The enemy is charming but deadly."

"You two, can we solve the world's big questions another day?" Lily asks. "We have to have a plan for tonight. What's first on your list, July?"

"We stay together. Six eyes are better than two. No one gets to sneak up on us. If attacked, we fight as a unit."

Khetiwe says, "Talking of fighting, let's check our weapons."

Lily makes a huff of impatience. I get up and collect my big jacket and empty the pockets, laying each item down on the sofa: knife, mobile, plastic ties, long nails, wire, flashlight, pliers, a screwdriver, and a small hammer. I don't empty the inside pocket. That's not their business. I say, "Number three: have easy access to mobiles and weapons at all times."

From her carry-all, Khetiwe produces a narrow black bum bag. "This is my mother's special international hidey bag. I 'borrowed' it. It can't be cut, torn, or burned. I have my knife, mace, fishing gut for cutting and tying, mobile, and a nail file. It's my miniature protection kit." She's proud of it. I like her confidence. It shows power.

Lily giggles. "With that around your waist you'll bulge like you have a spare tire."

Khetiwe nods. "That's why I wanted that red blouse. I left it on your bed. I'll get it when we change."

Lily says, "I have my knife, mace, and my mobile. I can fetch a hammer and nails from the garage, but I don't know where to find plastic ties. What are they for?"

"Tying people up. Put all your mobiles to vibrate, we don't want sudden renditions of Beethoven's Fifth giving away our hiding spots." I look meaningfully at Lily.

"Oh, that's my ring tone—how did you know?"

"Someone always phones you at first break," I reply.

"My mom. Okay. On vibrate, but that still makes a noise."

"It's the best we can do. Now we're ready for combat. On to number four: orientation. We need to know the house well enough to not get trapped in a corner. When we get there we'll have to walk around."

"I don't want to walk around, I want to stay with Darren," Lily gets up and pokes the fire, sending sparks flying up the chimney.

I lean back and stretch out my legs. When you're short, all chairs are too deep, too high. "I guess I can case the house by myself. You two stay close to Darren and Grant."

Khetiwe says, "But then you're in danger."

"Yes, but you aren't. I'll make a plan."

"No, Lily can stay with her brother. I'll come with you."

Lily growls in aggravation. "Fine, I'll come. But it's not the safest thing. I thought we have to stay safe."

"Number five, if you are in any danger, get out. Get out fast. Don't wait for anyone else. Always look after yourself first. There are no hero medals waiting for us."

Lily says, "If I find the rapist and he's with his victim, I know I'm going to try to help the victim, and then the rapist might escape or grab me. How do I not do that?"

"You've skipped down to number seven: be brave, not foolish. We're not the A-team, we're fifteen-year-old girls and we can die." They give me that bunny-in-the-headlights look again.

"The idea of knifing a human feels weird. I don't know if I can do it, even in self defense," Khetiwe says, playing with her knife. She's dexterous and quick.

"It does feel weird. Expect it to feel weird and if it happens, then it'll be what you expect," I tell her. "The first time someone punched me, I was so startled my brain froze. We don't expect to be hit by strangers. The random violence catapults us out of our childhood with its rules, and into the adult world that has no rules. It's disorienting. Like you're walking across a road, the road falls away and you're on a tightrope and there is no safety net. You have to get yourself to the other side. I thought I was going to die. Inside my brain fog, all I wanted was to survive. That's the most anyone can do."

As they each picture the event in their minds their expressions move from horror to concern and end in curiosity.

"Was it Andre?" Khetiwe asks. "What did you do?"

"I fell down unconscious. When I got home I bought a knife."

"Why would he hit you?" Lily asks.

"Because he could. He believed he would get away with it. Few people stop bullies."

"Did you go to the police?" Lily hugs her knees, drawing herself into a fetal position.

"Yes, I did. They said good girls stay at home. They blamed me."

"When I asked my father what a rapist looks like, after you told us to, he gave me a long look, and told me to call my mother," Khetiwe says. "I didn't learn anything, but it definitely got both my parents' attention. They've been watching me like hyper meerkats. It's like having a double full-beam radar on me all the time. They know I'm keeping secrets. I have to put them straight, they're so worried. They really didn't want me coming here or going out tonight. Tomorrow, I will tell them what we did and why."

Lily uncurls. "I asked my dad the same question. He said he doesn't see many rapists because women don't report rape.

Then he went to his study and closed the door."

"How does a judge square that with the statistics that every thirty seconds a woman or girl in South Africa is raped?" I ask. "How can tens of thousands of women be raped but no rapists are arrested by the police, charged, and brought to court? I'm not a judge but I can see something big is broken, and not for the good of women." I stare at Lily and raise my eyebrows, demanding an answer.

"I never thought about that," Lily says. "You're right, something is broken."

"And us girls are being cut on the sharp edges. How do we fix it?" Khetiwe asks.

I look at the fire slowly consuming the logs. "I think Mother Teresa said, 'We can't do great things; only small things with great love.' We respect and value ourselves and other women. We win every battle we're in. We fix what we can, like tonight. We grow up and become judges, police chiefs, prime ministers, politicians, and brigadiers of the Armed Forces. We take power, become the government, and change the law to benefit and build everyone in society. We've just lived through a revolution. We know how to do it, and it works." The logs shift, and more ash collects in the grate. I pull my eyes away from it and look across at the girls.

They're examining me like I'm a Picasso painting; all the right bits to make a human but no person in sight. Finally Lily says,

"You're a really good speaker. You never sound like this in English class. You must become a politician. I'd vote for you."

"Me too!" Khetiwe says smiling. "You have my vote and any other help I can give you."

I feel myself blushing. "Thank you. Deep question, deep answer." I sit up straight and shake my head. This luxurious room is lulling me into thinking I'm safe. I need to snap out of it before I spill my secrets. "Where were we? Back to number six: don't trust anyone."

"Except the people we know," Lily qualifies.

I look directly at her. "But maybe not their friends."

"What do you mean?" she asks. I brace myself to talk about Darren's friend.

The intercom buzzes. "Girls, are you getting ready? Darren's here."

Lily jumps up and hits the button. "We're on our way to my room now." She stays by the door. "Come on you two, we need to hurry, Darren's home. Time to dress. Come to my room, July."

"I have my clothes here." I don't want to change in front of them and reveal my scars.

"Just come!" She pulls at my arm. "We're a team now, we do things together."

I follow, thinking I'll come back and change once they're engrossed in their own dressing. I'll have to broach the topic of Lucas du Toit later. It's important. They must be warned, or at least alerted to a potential problem. Traitors are often our closest friends.

24. TIES THAT BIND

"JULY, WHAT SHOULD WE WEAR tonight to stay safe?" Lily asks, going to the wall of built-in wardrobes in her room; she opens all sixteen doors there. "I have something of everything, new and hand-me-downs from endless cousins." I can see she's proud of her clothes.

Khetiwe has already put on her chosen red blouse and is hunting among the skirts. "I'm thinking wide, medium length, easy to run in. What do you think, July?" She indicates a frothy silver skirt.

"Invisibility," I say, "we want to blend in. People don't notice you if you look exactly like they expect you to look. I'm wearing black jeans, a black hoodie and my big coat."

"Invisibility, really?" Khetiwe says. "Look at me!" She fluffs up her lighthouse-red hair. "I don't do invisible." She pulls on the skirt.

I laugh. "That's my point; everyone at the party will recognize your flashing ambulance-signal ball. It's what they expect, so they don't notice it anymore than I do. I'm talking clothes. Wear what they expect you to wear—but make sure you can run and fight in them."

Pulling a long, steel-handled comb through her mop she teases it even bigger. "Good! I brought a purse full of silver hairpins with tiny crystals on them." She pours them onto the dressing table. They gleam like diamonds. She didn't plan on being inconspicuous.

"Khetiwe, you and I will do a little glam." Lily says. "People will expect it, and we don't want my brothers wondering if we've lost our minds. And," she narrows her eyes at me, "I'll give those brown spikes of yours a makeover. I have a large tub of extra firm shimmer gel and a ton of hairspray, enough to tame that porcupine." Surprised, I brush my hand over my quills. They do feel especially pointy; last night hadn't included hair-washing.

"No," I say. "If you change my look I'll stand out like an elephant at a springbok convention. No one expects me to be glam. Most just hope I don't smell." They take a breath before laughing, embarrassed because I hit close to the truth. School lore: poor girls smell, so don't associate with them, don't get close enough to discover it's all a lie.

"You win that bet," Lily says to Khetiwe. "I tried and failed to polish July Abraham. Moving on, I have silver ballet flats that are glam and practical. Is that glamical? You want to try them?"

Khetiwe reaches for them. "Oh yes! I love having the same size feet as you. I can run in flats. No problem. I'll show you."

Lily hands over the shoes, then lifts a hanger with clothes from the back of her bathroom door and deposits it on her bed. "I'm going simple: black pants, a long-sleeved blue top, this long, dark blue boiled-wool jacket—it has deep pockets and is super warm—and then black runners, ugly but sensible." She puts them on and sits down at her dressing table to do her makeup. "If you want black jeans, Khetiwe, there's another pair on that shelf."

"Yes. I do. I'll be sensible like you." Khetiwe replaces her skirt with the jeans. "They fit like a dream. Look how well they go with the top." She pirouettes, making the top flow out in a circle. "No one will see my bum bag under this. The oodles of fabric hide everything. Now I need a jacket. What do you suggest, Lily?"

They act relaxed, cheerful, like girls preparing for a party.

I sit down on the chair by the window. "Can we talk about the man we're hunting?"

Khetiwe wheels around eyes alight, a long black wool coat in her hand. "Yes. Finally! What does a rapist look like? Tell me!" Lily nods and continues applying black eyeliner.

I check the bedroom door is closed; I don't want either of her brothers overhearing us.

"Well, here's what I've discovered. He's at all our parties and no one notices him, so he's not a stranger. I think he is an ex-pupil of Blue Ridge. We might even know him."

Khetiwe gasps. "Oh! I have information about him! I forgot to tell you. Andie said he was called Luke. She did! That's all she said she knew. Luke. She said someone said the rapist's name, and that the rapist wore something blue over his head. She said his eyes were blue. Lily, doesn't Darren have a friend called Luke?"

Lily turns to face us. Her quick brain has clicked down to the central idea circling the room, the unsaid implication, perhaps accusation.

"No! Darren's friend is called Lucas not Luke. He was a Blue Ridge prefect with Darren, and now he's a policeman. They acted in *Hamlet* together. Darren played Rosencrantz and Lucas Guildenstern. He's stayed here in this house many times. I know him. He's not a rapist. Darren is a great judge of character. He wouldn't have a rapist for a friend. How can you even think that?"

Khetiwe pulls the pin and throws the grenade. "The name Luke sounds a lot like Lucas."

Lily sits very still. Khetiwe looks at me as if I know what's going on. I shake my head and we both sit and watch Lily.

The eyeliner wand falls from her fingers on to the white carpet, making a mark. She doesn't notice. Is she having a black feathers moment? She's somewhere far away, reliving a memory. Her skin is paper white; lines crease her forehead as if she's worried. Had our description of Lucas du Toit opened a door long shut? My mom told me sexual abusers are usually people you know well, like family and close friends; people you can't get away from afterwards.

Khetiwe starts trying on the wool coat. I gesture, with palms down, for her to sit still. I don't want to scare Lily back to reality before she's ready. It's like waking a sleepwalker, I imagine. They get stressed and disoriented.

When Mom knew she was going to die, she pushed back the curtain on her past to share her wisdom. She'd been abused as a child. She emigrated to escape her tormentor. To explain her actions, she gave me statistics that showed globally two out of three girls are sexually abused by family members or close friends, and this unbroken chain of violence stretches back deep in time. Nursing, she saw a world made up of traumatized little girls who grew up to be silent, fearful women, and men who maintain the system. She pointed out that even though women paid taxes and made up fifty-two percent of the population, no war had ever been fought to stop a country that abused women. She refused to marry my father, because she believed a home with a man in it is not a safe place for any female. Her final gift to me was freedom through financially independence. My experience has proved my mother's views correct.

Is Lily back to being an abused little girl?

Khetiwe looks across at me and raises an eyebrow. She taps her watch. Time is passing, but I feel we must wait for Lily. I came back from my black feather moments, so will Lily.

It takes another minute before she sighs heavily, looks for her eyeliner wand and can't find it. She picks up her mascara brush instead and with an unsteady hand starts applying it. "Tell me what you think he looks like?" she asks.

I take her cue and carry on.

"Blond hair, blue eyes, tall, buzz-cut hair," I resurrect him as I speak, setting my teeth tingling with a familiar terror that tonight I will wipe from my life.

Lily gives a soft laugh. "You're describing both my brothers."

"Yes. I have, because he looks like them. Not just them, though. I have a list. Peter McNeil is on it, Johnny Dunst too."

Khetiwe snorts. "Peter McNeil is a creep; no respect for girls. All he wants is a brainless bimbo with puppy eyes. Now Johnny, he's sweet."

"But is he sweet when no one is watching him?" I ask. "We have to check each boy who fits the basic description: blond, blue eyed and buzz-cut hair."

"Johnny won't be there," Khetiwe says. "He never goes to parties." She's jogging on the spot in the glamical slippers. "These are great. I'm wearing them."

Lily says, "You must put Lucas du Toit on your blond boy list. Do you know that at school people thought Darren and Lucas were twins, or at least brothers? They did everything together. He was Darren's best friend. They still look the same, even though they don't try, like they did back then. And with Lucas a cop and Darren about to be a lawyer, they move in different circles, they don't see each other much."

Is Lucas being far away making Lily feel safe enough to remember? From her description I'm almost sure Lucas is the rapist, and I know, thanks to Andie, that I wasn't his only victim. At what age did he start hurting girls and found no one stopped him?

Lily turns around and smiles, fully present, eyes shining. "Yes! Let's go hunting. If it turns out to be Lucas, or any of Darren's friends, then they deserve what's coming to them."

I grin back. "Great! The more people in the hunt, the more

rats we catch. Eventually, we'll reduce the population."

There's a knock at the door and a man says, "Is it safe to come in?"

"Yes!" Lily shouts and jumps up to open the door to her brother. They hug. He smiles around at Khetiwe and me.

"You have a new friend. Introduce us." He walks over to me. Lily races beside him, saying, "This is July Abraham. July meet my brother, Darren."

He offers me his hand, and ice water freezes my veins, my body goes numb. I expected the blond hair and blue eyes. I didn't expect the round eye sockets that match exactly the face seared into my brain. Sweat forms on my brow, runs into my eyes. My arm and hand are solid, dead weights. I can't lift them. I won't touch that offered hand.

"Hi," I stammer through frigid lips. Can he feel the cold rolling off me?

He smiles, pretends he didn't notice the brush-off, and turns to Khetiwe. "That's a lot of diamonds. Is there someone you want to attract? I can grease the wheels."

Khetiwe laughs. "You noticed them. That's the whole point. They can be seen."

The intercom buzzes. "Grant is here. Are you all having a bite to eat before you leave?"

Darren presses the button. "Not me, Mom, I need to shower and get changed. See you ladies in about half an hour." He gives us a military salute and leaves.

Mrs Wesley says, "What about you girls? Shall I bring you coffee and buttermilk rusks?"

Lily replies, "Yes please, just come on in. We're in my room."

The intercom clicks off.

"She really wants to come and check on us. She's a natural worrier."

"She's amazing! I want her for my own mother," Khetiwe says, going back to the dressing-table mirror and adding six more pins to her hair.

I get up. I need a safe, quiet spot to nurse my jangling body. This cannot be a black feather night. "I'm going to change."

I check that the corridor is empty before I cross. I wish I could lock the door but Khetiwe might want to come in.

Collapsing on to the sofa, I stare at the fire. Love never dies, it turns to ash. A cloud of loneliness settles on me. What is the point of pushing on? I want the pain, the heaviness, the fear to end. I want to feel safe and loved. I don't want to think for myself every second of the day. I want to be with Mom. Sunk deep in my darkness, a thought taps me on the cheek: I forgot to check Darren's pinkie fingernails. What if it's not Lucas, what if it's Darren? I sit up, shaken.

"Mom," I whisper. "What if I select the wrong guy?" I wait while one tall orange flame licks hungrily at a log. The log pops out a shower of sparks.

"Mom! What do I do? I don't want to die. I don't want to be attacked again. That's why I have to do this. There's no other way. No one else cares. He must be removed. He hurts girls!"

"Keep yourself safe. I love you."

"Love you too Mom."

Knowing Mom is with me calms me. I change into my black clothes and recall Kevin saying, "Black doesn't make you invisible." At this party it won't matter. To stay close to Mom I sit down in front of the fire. More glowing logs burst into flames. I feel the rush of heat on my face. Fire burns. It's what it does. If we expect it not to, we're deluded. Cornered animals fight back. They want to survive. I am cornered fire. I will burn anything in my fight to live free of fear.

25. A HOUSE ON A HILL

THEY ARE SHORT, DARREN'S fingernails. He's driving and I can see both his hands. All his nails are clipped square. I don't think the rapist has clipped his nails. Why would he? They are part of his assault kit, and he still thinks he can attack with impunity. I don't trust Darren, even with the nail evidence. As a close friend of Lucas he must know what Lucas does and hasn't stopped him. That makes him an accessory.

I'm in the back of the car, squashed up against the door, with Khetiwe, Lily, and Grant. Shivers work their way through my body. Khetiwe can feel them. She pats my leg and gives me reassuring looks. It doesn't help; Darren is too close.

Lily keeps checking her pockets and Khetiwe her bum bag. We've all got serious faces and worry lines, like we're about to write a final examination, not attend a party. Fortunately Grant and Darren have Erin-centred tunnel vision. She's in the front passenger seat, her long black hair twisted in an intricate up-do with wispy side strands to show off her high cheek bones. Lily described Erin's dress as "almost there," and the parts that do exist won't keep her warm this Highveld winter night.

The headlights pick up clouds of red dust swirling lazily above the road. We're not the first people on this sandy track.

"Look up," Darren says. "Can you see those rows of lights on the hill? We're almost there. It's at the top of that hill."

"A house on a hill," I say. At first it looks like a spider's web of white lights, but then I pick out big, square lights marking the perimeter fence, and a second inner wall of smaller square lights. Within this, spherical lights follow erratic paths that converge on a large central building whose roof is covered in a net of small white lights. "It's a compound," I say thinking out loud.

"Sort of, it's one house spread all over the hill," Darren replies jolting me from my observations. "There's a story behind it. The first owner had seven sons. They all went to our school. The youngest matriculated a year ahead of me. Justin. Their Dad bought the land and said each son had to build his own living quarters. He supplied all the stuff, but they had to do the work. They could put their rooms wherever they liked; design them too. But they slept in the veld until their rooms were built. That three-storey central building the dad built for himself and his friends. Right at the top is the Great Room with a kitchen and living space, below it are guest bedrooms. Every time a son finished constructing their bedroom, the dad joined it to the central building with a passageway."

"What did their mother say about that?" Lily asks.

"Nothing, she died when Justin was little; a car accident."

"That's why the dad treated the boys so badly," Khetiwe says, "because he could."

"Why did they sell the house?" Erin asks. "It's unique."

"South Africa is unstable," Darren says, "white people living on plots and farms are big targets. The death rate is high. You can't give a plot away. Lucas got it for a steal. The owners immigrated to Australia. They even left behind their furniture."

"Did he buy it from the first owner?" Khetiwe asks.

"No. I don't know what happened to that family."

"What if we need to find the loo?" Erin asks. "Are they in any normal places?"

"There are lots of toilets. Every room is en suite, and there are guest toilets off the Great Room," Darren answers. "Don't hassle, you'll be fine. You won't get lost. Most of the people from our year are here. You'll be surrounded by friends."

Grant says, "And Lily, Khetiwe, and July stick with me. Mom wants me to keep an eye on you." He leans forward and gives me an extra hard stare. I wink at him. He shakes his head. When I want to get lost, I will.

We pass through the open security gate into a packed driveway. A stream of people weaves around the cars on their way to a stairway off to my left. I can hear music thumping. It's coming from the central building, which towers over us and is illuminated like a vertical runway.

"There's a parking space over in the corner," Grant says, "next to that red Toyota bakkie."

"Yes. Good! Here goes." Darren swings the car fast right, bumps off the drive and onto the veld and takes the spot. We're tossed about like a salad.

"See that green Golf coming in," Grant says, "that's Penny Harrods's car. Her brother Chris is in your class, Lily. I didn't know she'd be here." He sounds like he's interested in her. That might drop his interest in being our bodyguard. Darren's already lost to the mesmerizing Erin.

We exit the car and join the queue that's shuffling slowly towards the arched gates at the start of the stairway.

"I don't like Chris," Khetiwe whispers to Lily and me. "He's like gum on a pavement, nasty and yucky, teeming with infections."

"He has zero finesse around girls," Lily agrees. "He's like a big puppy who wees all over the place. He needs regular whacking with a rolled up newspaper."

Khetiwe laughs. "He needs fixing." She makes a snipping motion with her fingers.

"He's a good rugby player, plays that inside centre position really well," Grant says. "Watch, he and David McNeil will bring home that trophy tomorrow."

"Irrelevant!" Khetiwe says. "He's foul."

"If he comes near you, smack him straight in the gonads," Grant says. "That will activate his brain. If that doesn't work call me. I'll spell it out to him."

"Don't worry. If he steps out of line, I'll fix him," Khetiwe says, fastening her coat against the cold wind. Her ferocious tone makes Grant take a second look at her. I grin, impressed. She grins back and puts her hand on her hidden weapons bag. I give her a thumbs-up. The team is ready.

"Chris's folks, the Harrods, own a big computer business with branches all over Southern Africa," Erin says. "It's the one with that purple swirling sign in Menlyn. They're rolling in money."

Darren nods. "I've heard they have more money than the Van Buurens, but they don't flash it around. They live in a normal house in Lynwood, on the hill above Glenfair Mall. He could have gone to St Albans, the private all-boys school."

"I wish he had," Khetiwe says. "He has a one track mind and it's a dirt track."

Grant whistles. We all turn to see why. "It's Chris! He's driving his sister's car. He's only fifteen, he can't even have a learner's license. He's a total idiot!"

We watch Chris blithely park in front of one of the six bays of the garage, under the full beam of a security light. All other guests have left those spots for the family's use. Chris and David McNeil get out of the car, laughing.

"Peter told me David was grounded," Grant says. "Bet you he's bunked out. If he's caught, he won't play in the match. McNeil will see to that. Idiot! He'll cost the school a trophy, and for what?"

I get closer to Lily and whisper, "David told me he wasn't coming, and yet here he is. We need to watch him."

"Okay. Do we ask him why, or just observe from a distance?"

"If we get the chance to ask him, I'd be interested to hear his words."

Khetiwe joins us. "Someone's here in an ancient van, seriously, a real dinosaur. It's brown! Who would drive such an ugly monstrosity?"

We stop and stare at the brown Ford Transit bouncing its way towards the far garage.

I expected them, but seeing Richter's troops arrive is sobering. Tonight might be my last. I force down a lump in my throat and pull the girls out of the queue. Grant will hold our place.

"That is one of Richter's vehicles. Let's wait here and see who gets out."

Mpho Kageso parks the van. He, Andre Vermarck, and Leyton Donaldson climb out. With Richter's executioner up and running, I am in even deeper trouble than I thought. Forget blending in, I must disappear. I can't be seen with the girls. There goes rule number one.

"Richter isn't with them," Khetiwe says, her voice wobbles as the reality of the evening sinks in. There's nothing like seeing the enemy to bring the battle into focus.

"If they are here, he'll be here," I reply as I watch the threesome walk into the garage.

Grant calls, "Come on girls, we've reached the stairs, don't get left behind."

We hurry over to him.

"I bet no one volunteers to bring in the shopping inside this house," Khetiwe says, looking up the steep slope.

"They have a dumbwaiter to haul it up," Darren says, proving he is listening to our conversation.

"Can a person ride in it?" I ask, thinking of all the ways people get around this property maze.

"Maybe a child or a contortionist," Darren replies. "It's small;

they'd have to be motivated."

Lily is behind me. I drop back and whisper, "I can't come in with you. When we get near the top I'll change course and find a place to hide. One of Richter's dogs wants to kill me—long story."

"What about rule one, stay together? You can't leave now." She doesn't trust me. I can see it in her face. She thinks I've set her up.

"I can't help you if I am dead. I should have put Staying Alive first on the list. You and Khetiwe stick with Grant. As soon as I think I'm safe I'll join you."

"Do we keep looking for the boys on the list, or is that also over?"

I hear the sarcasm. I don't have time to soothe her nerves. "Always keep watching for the boys, and yes, do it from a safe distance. Don't let them see you. I'll get back as soon as I can. Stay safe."

I run down the stairs. I have no choice because stepping into that Great Room upstairs would be a life-shortening event. Reaching the driveway, I head towards the garage. I want to see the dumbwaiter.

26. INTELLIGENCE

ALL SIX BAY DOORS to the garage are closed. No one is around keeping watch. Is Richter short-staffed tonight? Debating what to do next, I hear voices. Chris Harrods and David McNeil come around the corner. I run out across the driveway to the parked cars and hide behind one.

"Well look who's here," David says. I swing around, heart pumping erratically, thinking they've sneaked up on me.

"Yes, why are you here?" That's Lily's voice. Why is she here? She shouldn't be here. She must have followed me down the stairs and, worse, I didn't notice. Now we are both in danger from any free-ranging Richter goon.

"I'm looking for you two and July," David replies.

You two? Did he say two? Who else is here? They are well hidden, standing outside the umbra of the garage lights. I creep forward in search of answers. Ignorance is dangerous.

"Come on, Davie," Chris says. "Forget July, let's bag these honeys and leave the feral cat alone. They don't like bags."

"No. I came for all three."

Chris growls in frustration.

"What does that mean?" Khetiwe asks. "You came for us. What are you two up to?"

Khetiwe is also here? Now I get it, they chose to stick with me even though I explained the danger. They put the team first; they are team players. Again their concern for me warms my heart. They are right, we must stay together. I stand up and walk over to them.

Chris whistles. "Speak of a fright night, here's the lead non-honey zombie. Davie boy, we have a full house. Let's throw them in the car and *waai*. Job done."

"Answer Khetiwe," I tell David, easing my hoodie further over my head in case anyone looks our way. "Why are you here? What are you two up to?"

"We've come to take you away. Let's go, we've got Penny's car." David sounds like he believes he's handing out free money and we want it.

"Who died and left you in charge?" Khetiwe asks. Lily and I glare at him until he finally registers that we're not eager, grateful Labrador puppies ready to jump in his car and go for a walkies.

"What? No! Wrong. You've got it all wrong. Listen up. This is a rescue mission. This is a good thing. There's a rapist here! I don't want to be blamed if anything happens to you like with Andie. Folks said I should have protected her. So here I am protecting you by taking you home."

"You listen up," I say. "We planned to be here. We came with Lily's brothers. Did Peter come with you?" He's dressed in a rugby track suit and dirty runners, even worse party clothes than mine. Chris looks like he's wearing pajamas, but then no one expects more of him. Maybe their rescue story is true; maybe it's a great deception.

"What? Peter? No. I don't know. I didn't hear his plans. I came to get you to safety and then get home before my dad finds out I'm AWOL and bans me from playing tomorrow. Chris offered to supply the car. Please come. I don't have much time." He points to the car. Chris jingles the keys. I resist the urge to grab them and throw them over the fence. Let Chris go fetch, it'll take his mind off us.

"David, you don't decide what we do," Lily says as she walks over to me. Khetiwe follows her. David looks bewildered.

"But July said us men have to stand up against rapists. This is me doing that. Don't you want to be looked after?"

Lily sighs loudly, Khetiwe rolls her eyes, and I shake my head.

He looks at me. "What? It's a great offer."

"We're not buying what you're selling. Let me explain. To fight a rapist you need to stand in front of a rapist. Is the rapist one of us girls?" I wait until he shakes his head. "Well then, why are you here? Don't lock up girls because there is a rapist about, lock *him* up. If you make girls hide away, then you give rapists an excuse. They see a girl outside and believe they can rape her for being outside."

Exasperated, Chris says, "Davie, don't argue with the fright-night zombie. She's nuts. Dagga-fried brains. Let's bag them, stick them in the car, and make this happen. Time's a ticking." He lunges at me. I knee him in the gonads. He hits the ground hard then curls, groaning into a ball. I back up ten steps, pulling Khetiwe and Lily with me. They look scared, expecting the worst. Lily already has her phone in her hand.

Chris croaks, "Shit, Davie, why did you choose a Crazy for your honey?"

David blushes and turns to me. "So a no-go? What do we do then to keep you all safe?"

"Do what July told you," Lily says. "Find the rapist and hand him over to the police." She points at Chris, "And keep him away from us."

He helps Chris up. "Got it, we're on our way."

"Easy for you to say," Chris grumbles limping after his friend.

We huddle up as the boys leave. Lily giggles, which sets Khetiwe off, who says, "I've wanted to smash that creep for ages and now you did! Well done!"

"He needs to learn he can't grab people," I say. "Do you want to do a bit of snooping, now that we're down here and there's no one watching the garages? We could look for the back stairs and the dumbwaiter."

"No!" they speak together. Chris's aggression has unsettled them.

"You know that Chris isn't going to come and hurt us? He's very clear now on what he can and can't do."

"I felt scared," Khetiwe says. "I expected him to get up and hit us. Isn't that why we run away and try not to get into fixes, so we don't have to say no? I always thought saying no provoked them and saying no made it my fault."

"It's not your fault. Boys are responsible for their own actions. Everyone has the right to say no." I'm beginning to sound like my mom; it pleases me.

"I understand what Khetiwe means," Lily says as we begin to climb the stairs. "I don't think I've ever felt allowed to give a straightforward no to a male. I choose less direct words and back away. Somehow I know deep down that saying no is dangerous, that I'll get hurt and blamed. Until tonight I never thought to question it. As I step on each of these stairs I keep repeating 'I have the right to say no' and each time I hear the reply, 'Are you sure?'"

"You do," I say. "Believe it. That doesn't mean those with the power won't fight back. No one gives up power easily, but their anger doesn't take away your human right to say no."

We fall silent, each wrapped in our chosen coat of thoughts. Mine is thick and heavy with plenty of pockets for all the weapons I need. I think Lily's is form-fitting leather, unique and durable. Khetiwe's is a double layered cloak, sparkling and attractive on top, weatherproof, warm, and tough underneath. We're a stronger team than I ever thought we'd be.

Lily's mobile vibrates. "Grant is looking for us. We have to go straight up to the Great Room. He's annoyed that we just disappeared without telling him. He called me irresponsible. What cheek! I'm always responsible. That's why I got Khetiwe to come with me to be with you. We agreed to fixed rules. No changes midstream."

Khetiwe shivers. "I can't wait to be inside and warm."

I follow behind them, rethinking my plan to hide from Richter's gang. Everyone already knows I'm here. Surely I'll be safe with the girls and Grant. If I feel threatened, I'll disappear. By then I'll have had more sense of the room and its hiding places.

27. FIRST BLOOD

MPHO KAGESO IS IN THE KITCHEN, sipping beer from a can. I slip behind the floor-to-ceiling wall of black curtains. There are cracks between each section, giving me a view over the room. I try to avoid them. If I can see someone, then maybe they can see me. My black-booted feet stick out, marking my position like dots under exclamation marks. I slide along until I'm behind an unoccupied spindly wooden chair—one of those designer creations, all right angles and discomfort, and probably worth tons of money. The room is warm. Cheerful kwela music rises above the laughter, conversation, and cigarette smoke. Tea-light candles in deep glass vases complement the soft mood lighting.

The chair creaks. Someone is close. I hold my breath and squeeze back against the window.

"Is that you?" Lily asks. I breathe out in relief.

"Yes. Was it my boots? Did they give me away?"

Khetiwe says, "No. We came over because you said we'd find you behind a curtain. We've walked the whole wall stopping everywhere, as if talking to a curtain is exactly why we came to this party. I'm sure everyone thinks we're nuts."

"No one is interested in us," Lily says. "Look at Grant, he's so happy chatting with Colleen, Peter McNeil's official girlfriend. She's a sweetie. She should switch to Grant, he's way better than Peter. I wouldn't want a guy who hangs with all girls. How does that make you special?"

"Is Peter a good guy?" Khetiwe asks. "Can we take him off our list?"

"I don't know yet. It's too soon," I reply. "Mpho is monitoring the room. The rest of the gang is here, but invisible. Where are they collecting?"

"Well, in a house designed like this one, the party will split into cliques and go anywhere," Khetiwe says. "Why hang with folks you don't like when you don't have to?"

I was afraid of that. How do I infiltrate Richter's clique? The simple and only answer is I can't. By definition cliques are small, exclusive, tightly locked. Then again, zebra hang in zebra cliques and lionesses eat them. We must hunt like lionesses, winnow out the weakest, one by one, until we've consumed the herd. The weakest right now is Mpho Kageso. He's alone and feels secure. We have the element of surprise. I'm about to launch my plan to the girls when Lily says,

"July, do you trust David?"

"Rule six, don't trust anyone," I reply. "Where's Mpho Kageso right now?"

"I can't see him, but David and Chris are collecting beers from the fridge."

Kageso's gone. He might be reporting my sighting to his boss. Now I'm the prey. I feel a prickle of panic. I have to move, hide. Where?

"Both are fully untrustworthy," Khetiwe says, "And David's brother is too smooth."

"Shush! David's coming over," Lily says, then I hear David.

"Hi again, just another check, can I take either of you home?"

"Go away," Khetiwe replies.

"Where is July?" he asks. "You girls must stick together."

I want to step out, move with the team, but I don't fully trust David because of his brother, so I stay where I am.

"Go away," Lily says.

"Listen," he says. "This is serious. It's dangerous here. Lily, go tell one of your brothers about the rapist. There's Darren. Tell him. When he knows, he'll take you out of here so fast your head will spin. If you don't, I will."

"Why would you do that?" Lily asks. "What do you gain by doing that?"

"Your safety. Don't move. I'm going to find July, she mustn't be here alone."

Khetiwe says, "Well what do you make of that, July? I think the boy likes you."

"And he's more persistent and irritating than a mosquito," Lily adds. I imagine her rolling her eyes. Then a draft of cold air opens up behind me, someone grabs my arm and pulls me backwards across the brick paved deck.

"July Abraham, the boss wants to see you again," announces Andre Vermarck, pulling me off the deck and around to a set of cement steps.

I twist, kick, punch, and finally bite him. He slaps my face and grabs my ear, forcing my head down towards my knees, every muscle from my mouth to my eyeballs tenses with the strain. One snaps; I hear the ping, and then the molten burn. The pain is excruciating. My jaw aches like I've lost a tooth. I swallow a scream. He's on my left, moving us fast down the stairs. I'm off balance. I can't get my feet under me. Using every abdominal muscle I have, I lift my left foot, bring it forward and put it on the ground. It acts like a break. The interruption to his stairs rhythm almost trips him up.

"Bitch!" He kicks my foot.

Pain shoots through my shin and up my leg. I ignore it. I know what to do. Bent over like this, my hand is close to my coat pocket, as are his ankles. I ease my knife out. Using all my strength, I place both my feet on the ground, wait for him to stop then I lunge forward and slash at his heels. I hit his right ankle clean. Blood spills. He gives a scream, lets go of me, grabs at his heel, hobbles two steps, and falls.

I head up the stairs until I register that someone is chasing me. I can hear his panting. He can hear me panting. He's climbing fast. I must change direction.

I step to the right, off the path on to uneven veld, and climb up towards the nearest patch of darkness. The ground flattens out. I brush against sharp leaf shrubs and blackjack bushes. My foot connects with rock and I fall to my knees into what feels like a sand pit. I roll over and stop. Now what? Which direction is safer? If he finds me he will kill me, or take me to the rapist, who will do worse. I scrabble straight across the sand and climb out on to a flat lawn. The house is to my right, lit up like a beacon of hope. I can see the crowded Great Room, people dancing and laughing, oblivious to any problem. If I try to return to the party and make it to the house alive, how long before the gang grabs me again? Do I get the choice?

I hear the crack and rustle of undergrowth as someone closes in on me.

No. I don't get the choice. Kevin said they planned to silence me tonight, and Kevin has always played it straight with me.

My heart thuds in my chest, my teeth zing and buzz in my gums. My face aches.

I'm such an idiot. How unaware was I to stand at a window, like a mannequin in a shop, the deck lights shining right on me? My first instinct had been to hide and not go in that room. Why did I not follow my own good sense? It's the pull of the group. I felt safe in my team, smugly thinking, "I've got this." I relaxed my guard and bang, they hit me. Lesson learned. I already know that dying is an individual activity; you figure it out alone.

Here in this crazy maze of a house, the rapist holds all the aces. This lawn could be exactly where he's prepared a special welcoming committee for me. I pull my mind away from the faces of the boys who stood around watching him rape me that Friday: Leyton Donaldson, Andre Vermarck, Travis Richter, and Mpho Kageso. I didn't fight that time. I didn't believe anyone would treat me that way. I expected someone to yell, Stop! I thought everyone was essentially good. I was wrong. People do whatever they can get away with. They back off when you fight. I'm no longer naive. I fight.

On the far edge of the lawn, I see the triangular shapes of fir trees. Keeping to the dark outer edge of the lawn, I move cautiously towards them. Picking one, I find its branches too tightly packed together for climbing. I wiggle under its lowest branches and hook my legs around its rough trunk. The scent of pine carries me back to the night I found Andie. I survived that night and saved her, now I must save me. Holding my knife firmly I prepare for battle. This is not a game of tag. This is a gladiatorial event. He intends to kill me and I intend to stop him.

In the Media Centre earlier, preparing for this night I had read about fear and discovered that fearlessness is a myth. Fear is one of our animal survival instincts. To get beyond fear, like a snake I must shed the old, small, scared July, and replace her with a new, strong me. In the warmth of that booklined sanctuary I couldn't imagine how to achieve this, but here in this cold spiky reality I know what I must do—survive the fight. If I live I will have time to think about how I did it.

"African Sky Blue" by Johnny Clegg begins playing in the Great Room. It might as well be on Saturn, I can't get there and no one inside will hear me scream. Where are the girls? Are they looking for me? I hope they don't try to take on one of the gang. I don't want their deaths on my conscience, not now, seconds before I might meet God.

It's too quiet. He must be close, or has someone less puffed taken over the hunt? Is it a relay race for them, each handing over the baton to the other? Perhaps they have a sentry out here who's been tracking me the whole time?

I hear a sudden intake of air. I tighten my grip on my knife. Something hits a branch above me, showering me with fir needles. Not a bullet, a rock. I taste blood. I've bitten my tongue.

Strong hands grab my shoulders and start pulling me from under the tree. I hold on tight to the trunk, ignore the pain of bark tearing through my jeans and into my legs. I push the button and expose my knife blade. A boot digs in next to my elbow. Inside a leg is a big artery, easier to reach from the back. If I cut it he will have to let go of me. I feel down the leg until I think I have the spot then I slam in the blade. Blood soaks my fingers. I don't know how deep I must press, but I'll keep going until he stops fighting.

With a groan my attacker attempts to smash my hand away. The low branches block him. He punches me in the face. The shock runs down through my neck and shoulder. I don't need to see, I need to hold on and get my blade in as deep as possible. I am determined to inflict as much damage as I can in whatever time I have left. I will put this girl-hurter out of action for as long as possible. Stars flash across my eyes. A vicious punch to the left side of my face stuns me, but I hang on, like a limpet on a rock; unaffected by rough waves at high tide. I will live. Finally he crumples to a heap and releases me. Pulling out my knife, I roll away and break free of the tree.

I feel like yelling, "VICTORY!" I'm shuddering with the effort and I can't feel my legs, my head feels askew on my neck, but I don't care, I AM ALIVE! My blood is racing at 5000 kilometres per hour around my body making every hair stand erect and tingle, outlining me as if to celebrate my existence, prove that I occupy space on this planet, show that I do count, I am valued and wanted. I feel larger and stronger. I have shed my small skin and am now a warrior. The universe is on my side.

The cold air bites. I'm sweating and shivering, the drying blood sticks my fingers together. It occurs to me that I still don't know who I fought. I fumble in my pocket for my flashlight. Before I can free it a shadow emerges and crawls towards me. Instantly on guard, I take a firm grip on my knife and prepare for round two. I'm not scared anymore. The thought of fighting is exhilarating, like freewheeling a bike down a steep hill. You do it again and again for the joy of the wind rush and the freedom from gravity.

"July?" Khetiwe whispers, holding her can of mace ready. I let out my breath and relax my knife arm.

"Yes." I leopard-crawl over to them.

Khetiwe and Lily hunker down next to me. Khetiwe shines her light over onto my attacker's face. Leyton Donaldson, Richter's hit man. I'm thrilled. The worst battle is over and I started not with a lame duck, but with the strongman.

"It's not Andre Vermarck," Khetiwe whispers in surprise.

"No, why would it be?" My lips burn as I speak. They must be split.

"Because we followed him out here," Khetiwe explains looking around. "He's also out here."

Now I'm on high alert. You don't need a good ankle to kill someone, you just need a loaded pistol and Andre has that.

"I'm glad you're alive," Lily says and touches my arm. "What's this wet stuff?"

"Blood. Come on. We need to get away from here. Andre has a pistol. He will kill us."

"Follow me," Khetiwe says, standing up. "I saw a room just across the lawn, off to the right of the Great Room. See— there's a path. Those bushes hide most of it, except the roof. We can keep cover along this line of trees until we reach the path almost at the door."

I struggle to stand and hear myself grunting in pain. It feels like I've dislocated my hip. Also, my right shoulder is too close to my chin. My face is crooked and heavy. I have mono-vision. This level of agony is new to me. Lily puts her shoulder under mine and lifts me. A moan escapes me. I clamp shut my mouth, determined to stay silent while we are still in danger. Khetiwe takes the other side and we move forward as a team.

"Good thing you're short and seriously lightweight," Khetiwe says with a laugh. "I don't usually carry people around."

Lily says, "Do we leave Leyton out here? Should we call someone?"

"Whoever sent him will come and find him," I croak. "That's why we need to get out of here before that happens."

Johnny Clegg's song "Bullets for Bafazan" comes on and we watch as Travis Richter, in a tuxedo, begins gum-boot dancing to an appreciative audience. We don't say what we all think, how come no one takes him down when he is right in front of them?

28. CLEAN-UP

THERE IS A TINY RED LIGHT flashing above the bedroom door. I stop.

"See that light? It's like the listening camera you have at your house, Lily. What if it alerts someone to our arrival?"

"I'll go in and check?" Khetiwe offers.

"No! Once you're in, it's too late. They have you. I'm going to follow my gut instinct and avoid this place. Let's go to the lower level of the main house and find a bathroom in one of the guest-rooms."

We change course. I pull my hoodie over my head and Khetiwe and Lily form walls on either side of me shielding me from prying eyes. Fortunately, in the dark depths of the big house, the couples are more interested in sucking face and rubbing nubs than staring at us.

Lily tries several doors before finding an empty bedroom. We lock ourselves in and head straight into the bathroom and lock that door too. It's a large bathroom with a separate shower and tub.

I ease myself down on to the edge of the tub. Across from me, in the mirror above the basin, I see a twisted balloon-faced, blood-caked monster. It startles me. Yet the girls hid their revulsion when they first saw me. They are powerful people. They make me feel stronger.

I lick my torn lips and say, "I'm going to shower and let the water rinse off the blood."

"And, now that I see you in the light, we have to talk First

Aid," Khetiwe says, putting down the lid of the toilet and sitting down. "Your face needs cleaning, and definitely stitches." She raises her eyebrows, inviting Lily to comment.

Lily walks up to me and examines my face. "Oh! This is bad! Khetiwe is right. That tear needs stitches. I'm phoning Darren. You have to go to hospital." She takes out her phone.

"No, no, wait. Just give me a chance. I want to finish what we came here to do. I'll survive until then." Like a contortionist slipping silently out of heavy chains, I ease off my jacket without lifting my shoulder. Pain engulfs me and I make a noise even I can't identify. The girls shake their heads at me.

"July! Come on! Don't be silly!" Khetiwe says. "There's a large flap of flesh on your face. Deep wounds must be closed within a fixed time limit, after that they can't be stitched or even stapled. You'll end up with a horrible scar, especially if it gets infected. You must go to the hospital."

Lily leans forwards. "July, you're in shock. Let us make the important decisions right now. You can't even walk. I'm phoning Darren. Wash your hands and we'll go." I hear her fear. She has a point. They must leave. It's not their fight. I'm being unfair risking their lives.

"Tonight is over. Accept it," Khetiwe says. "We'll try again another time."

"And I don't want to be here anymore," Lily adds. "You're my guest after all. How will I explain this to my mom?" She waves her hand from my head to my feet. "She'll have a meltdown. I'll be grounded forever."

"I don't have to come home with you. That way your mother won't see me. I'll organize another ride. This isn't your fault. We were attacked. This is not our crime. If you want to phone Darren, do it. I'll stay here. I'm not completely unable. I just need a rest. Hey, I can hitch a ride with Chris Harrods." Their eyes widen and their jaws drop in horror.

"You can't do that," Lily says. "If you won't go, we won't go. We stay together."

"You need us," Khetiwe explains, "you move like a robot with a flat battery and missing parts."

Lily phones Darren. "I have to go home now. It's serious. Yes, they want to come with me. What? No! This is really important someone's . . . " She looks up at us. "He hung up. He says I'm being whiny and his solution is that we join him. Leigh-Anne du Toit has a whole sub-party going. I'm sorry July. He wouldn't take me seriously."

"Maybe Chris is our best bet. At least we'd get you to a hospital," Khetiwe says, dejectedly.

I empty my outer pockets on to the counter next to the basin. "It seems the universe is saying, don't give up now. I'll get cleaned up and we can reassess the situation." Taking off my boots and socks I slip the contents of my inner pockets into them. Dizzy and stiff, I shuffle over to the shower leaving a pink snail trail in my wake. I close the frosted glass door behind me. Undressing involves carefully easing parts of my clothing out of my mangled flesh. I toss them out on to the bathroom floor. I hear cupboard doors opening and closing.

Lily says, "I've found soap and a black towel." Her hand comes into the shower and I take the soap. "I'm going to look in the bedroom cupboards to see if there are any clothes there for you. Hey! Found Dettol, cotton wool balls, sanitary towels, and plasters, we can patch you up. Khetiwe—hand July this bottle of shampoo."

An opened bottle of shampoo is placed on the shower floor.

"Jackpot!" Lily shouts. "Men's shirts, jackets, trousers, pants, socks, and belts. Size 34. Too big for you, July, but we can make them work."

I turn on the shower taps and a jet of cold water hits my face, pulls down my torn flesh. White lightning flashes across my brain. Red water swirls around my toes. I can see deep gashes running down from my knees to my ankles. It's hard to stand up straight, but I hope the warm water will help. Lowering my head to knee height, I shampoo my hair. There's a large, bald spot on my head. That explains the skull ache. I rinse, turn off the taps, and wrap myself in the towel and step out.

Khetiwe and Lily both look concerned when they see me.

"As we can't get you to a hospital, I will play doctor," Khetiwe says. "I have my Red Cross badge, and Lily has found a first aid bag with tons of little plasters."

"Did you find any painkillers?" I ask Lily. "I need about a hundred, extra strength."

"No. I'll keep looking." She goes out into the bedroom.

"Come, sit," Khetiwe says, laying out her tools on the counter next to the basin. I take the stool in front of the basin and look in the mirror. What can she do with this purple, blue, and broken monster? She's confident and calm.

"If you are going to get stitches I can't disinfect the wound, but you've rinsed it, so now I can pinch the edges together and hold them in place with these tiny plasters. You'll look like Frankenstein's monster, but it might save your face. Then I'll clean the rest with Dettol."

She's gentle and deft, fully absorbed in her task.

"You'll make a great doctor."

She smiles. "I'm planning on being a surgeon. What do you want to be?"

"The owner of my own billion rand company. I need a BCom, an MBA, and some great ideas." I've never told anyone that. How will she react?

"I can see you doing that. You're great at accounting. You make it look easy, and you always have the highest marks." She finishes my face and begins disinfecting my other wounds.

I stare at myself in the mirror. "You've done a great job. But, you're right my party is over, unless I stay in the dark and away from all people." I run my fingers through my hair trying to cover the gap.

Khetiwe says, "I think we need to eat humble pie, phone David, and accept his help."

"Yes. You're right. I'm facing the facts and they're ugly." We both stare at my face in the mirror. Can she see past the wounds to the pain and fear in my eyes, maybe even the defeat?

"I'll phone David once you're dressed. Where did you learn to fight like that? Pretty awesome." She puts the top on the Dettol bottle.

"My mom and I took self-defense classes."

Lily returns. "No painkillers in these rooms. Who's vibrating?"

"Me," Khetiwe answers then covers the microphone and whispers, "its David. Shall I ask him?" Lily and I both nod. She turns to the phone. "Can we get a ride home? You lost Chris? He's left? Maybe or not. Does your brother have a car? No. A sub-party in Leigh-Anne's rooms. Everyone from our school. Okay, see you." She turns to us.

"Seems we're stuck here. He says to go to this sub-party, its safe, but how can we go there? July . . . " They stare at me.

"Don't look at the negative," I say. "You two can still go there and talk to Darren and David. Convince one of them to take you home, and while you two organize our getaway, I'll stay here and get dressed. I might even try out the bed."

They shoot me dirty looks.

"We'll help you dress. You need us. We're not going anywhere without you," Lily says.

Fifteen minutes later, I look like a clown. My grey dress pants have huge folded hems, the silk magenta paisley shirt, cinched by a belt, falls to my knees, and a knitted beanie covers my damaged hair. I pull it down low. In an attempt to hide this fashion nightmare, Khetiwe loans me her long black coat. My dirty clothes are stuffed into a backpack that Lily found.

I sit down on the bed. "Time for you to go. According to David's directions, Leigh-Anne du Toit's room is at the very end of this same corridor. You can phone me when you're ready to leave."

"Okay," Lily says stacking pillows behind me, "But we won't be long. Keep your phone in your hand."

Khetiwe pulls the bedcover over my lap. "Phone for any reason. Any!"

"Yes. If you find any painkillers bring them with you."

They leave.

I get up and lock the door. Leaning back on the pillows I reevaluate my plans. No more quick evasive tactics, running, or fights. If I still want to put the rapist out of action I have to play it safe and smart. But do I still want to? I'm tired, sore and, yes, scared. I don't want to die. That thought wakes me up to my task. If I don't get him he'll kill me and continue to hurt more girls.

My phone vibrates.

Khetiwe says, "Just checking you'd answer! Leigh-Anne doesn't have just a bedroom, it's a whole huge apartment. Everyone is here: David, Peter, Darren, Grant, and most of the matric girls."

I can hear the laughter around her. "Great! Did you ask Darren for a ride home?"

"Not yet. He's with Peter McNeil. As soon as they finish talking I'll ask. You rest."

"Oh, hang on, Khetiwe, is Lucas there?" I might as well know where my enemy is.

"You and Lily both think the same! She asked Grant and he said Leigh-Anne told him Lucas is working tonight, he'll be home later."

"Thanks. Phone me as soon as you are ready to leave. Stay

close to Lily, and don't trust anyone even in that sweet safe spot."

"Will do! Bye!" We disconnect.

I don't intend to go with the girls. I just want them safely out of the way.

I wait ten minutes. My phone doesn't ring. The girls must be enjoying the party. I'm glad for them. While they are safe, I'll do some exploring of my own.

With Leyton and Andre out of the picture, and Lucas not expected until later, I need to locate Richter and Mpho. If I'm watching them they can't sneak up on me, and I don't need them blocking the way to my target. There is a pathway from the lower level of this house to the main outside stairway and at least three pathways from there to the garage. One of them must end up at the bedroom that is being used by the gang.

29. LOYALTY

I HOBBLE DOWN THE STAIRS like the hunchback of Notre Dame, hoping the movement will loosen my muscles and return me to normal; it doesn't. Every jolt pushes pain's fingers deeper into my body. To catch my rapist, he'll need to be sedated and caged.

Following one of the back pathways I arrive at the rear end of the garage and see a door leading into the garage. Before I test the door, I walk around to check that no one is standing guard at the front of the bays. The last bay door is open and Mpho Kageso is sitting in the brown van.

I step back into the bushes lining the pathway.

Mpho Kageso gets out of the van, locks all the doors, and then walks past my hiding place and heads behind the garage. I follow him. He turns left onto a smaller path and I hear him climbing steps. Then a light goes on in a window above me, indicating yet another bedroom.

I go over to the brown van, take the hammer and four long nails from my pocket, and tap them into the front and rear tires. There is a satisfying hiss of air. Tonight, their drug pantry is going nowhere.

My phone vibrates. The girls must be ready.

"Yes?" I whisper, but hear nothing. I end the call and phone Lily. She doesn't answer. I phone Khetiwe, same thing. Spurring my reluctant legs into an ungainly jog, I duck through the entrance arch and climb the main stairs to the house.

My brain tosses out scenarios. I told them to stay with

Darren. Darren means Lucas. Lucas means . . . no! Darren wouldn't allow his own sister to be assaulted, would he? But what about Khetiwe, she's not a sister. Sisters! Lucas has a sister—Leigh-Anne, of epic sub-party fame, who told Darren that her brother wasn't here. What if she lied? What if she works with Lucas to supply him with girls? Girls trust girls. No one would suspect her at all. I didn't, all I saw was an airhead fawning over Peter McNeil. Mom said families hide their secrets; everyone has to toe the line; sisters protect their brothers, regardless of how vile their brothers are. And I handed Khetiwe and Lily over to Leigh-Anne. I have put them in danger. Now I have to save them.

The door to Leigh-Anne's bedroom is wide open. There is no one here. No music. A sports' commentator is talking rugby on the television. Someone is coming down the passage. I move inside the room and hide behind the door.

David McNeil appears carrying two sixpacks of beer. He stops in the doorway and looks bewildered. Swinging around, he peers down the passageway then steps into the room, drops the packs of beer onto a chair and takes out his phone.

"Hey, yes, where'd you all go? Why? Why didn't you tell me? No. Shit! You're a total jerk." He pockets his phone; opens one of the beer packs, and helps himself to a can. Before he opens it, I slam closed the door behind him.

He swirls around, drops his drink, fists tight and ready to fight, then relaxes. "Oh, you. Whoa! What the hell happened . . . did the rapist grab you? Who did that to you? Is that what Khetiwe meant? I'll track down Chris and get you out of here."

"Stop! You're blabbering. And don't phone yet. Listen first. I came for Khetiwe and Lily. Where are they?"

He picks up the beer can and takes a sip. "Peter said Leigh-Anne told everyone to go up to the Great Room to dance; there's more space there and a better sound system."

"Did Khetiwe and Lily go? I mean you told them to come to Leigh-Anne's room and you promised to look out for them." I know we told him to get lost, but if it motivates him to action I'll use it.

Looking serious, he makes a call. "Peter says Khetiwe and Lily aren't there. He's not sure if they came up or went someplace else."

"Was Grant with them last time you saw them?" I ask surveying the room.

"Yes. Everyone was here. Peter sent me to get more beer."

"That's upstairs. How come you didn't see all these folk arriving?"

"There's a short cut from here to the main floor pantry. I used the back stairs."

I walk into the kitchen, bedroom, and bathroom. David follows me, even into the bathroom. I turn on him.

"Out! No place for you in here." He blushes and backs away.

I examine every cupboard and even inside the shower. No one there, but I find a box of Panados and a tube of Vaseline. I take four of the painkillers and gulp them down with tap water. The Vaseline is a blessed balm for my lips. I pocket the box and the tube; it's the small things that empower you to keep going.

Returning to the bedroom, I crouch down and look under the bed—nothing. When I open the cupboard doors, I find women's clothing and decide to ditch my clown suit. Selecting a shirt and a pair of jeans, I return to the bathroom to change, hanging the men's clothing on a hook on the bathroom door. I keep Khetiwe's coat, it has pockets with all my weapons and now the painkillers and tube. I hear David's phone ring and leave the bathroom to listen.

"Oh . . . no we haven't. July . . . ? She's here with me."

"Is that your brother?" He nods and stares at the phone, mouth pursed, wondering, what? Does he also not trust his brother? "He wants to know where you think the girls are. Should I tell him what we're both thinking?"

"That the rapist has taken them. Ask him and Colleen to go down to the driveway and make sure no vehicle leaves the area. If he finds the girls he must phone you." David relays the message and obviously gets an earful.

"He's phoning the police. He says wait for them."

"He can, I'm not. The police are a clean-up squad; they always arrive after the event. Five minutes ago I watched Mpho Kageso set the van up for a delivery. He's Richter's driver. He's expecting a cargo, I think they intend to leave here with the girls. I've flattened the tires on the van, but they have other cars. We must stop all vehicles from leaving. Can we close the gates? No one in or out until we find them."

David shares this with Peter, then tells me, "He's on his way."

"Good. Can you phone Grant Wesley for me?"

He dials the number then hands me the phone. "You go ahead, skip the middle man."

"Hey, Grant, July here. Is Lily with you? No. Remember Andie Elliot. Yes, the girl who was raped . . . I think the rapist has your sister and Khetiwe. Tell Darren. Thanks." I return the phone and walk to the door. The painkillers are kicking in, I can almost walk upright.

"Come. We have to hurry." I leave Leigh-Anne's apartment, walk down the corridor and see a black metal door to my right, unlike the white, wooden bedroom doors. "Is this a short cut up to the pantry?" I ask, noticing he's left his beer behind.

"No, that one is further down. I don't know where this one goes."

It opens to a cement staircase going both up and down.

Finger to my lips I gesture for David to stay silent and whisper, "Let's go down and see where we end up."

"Both of us?" he whispers.

I nod. "And you go first. Walk fast, don't talk. Be alert."

"It's a good thing I trust you," he says. "I don't have to worry about you locking me in here."

"Don't trust me," I tell him, checking my knife is safely in my pocket.

30. TRACKING

IT IS MORE THAN A STAIRCASE, it's an artery of a central nervous system—a network of tunnels and staircases. The house leans into a hill and is a warren. We creep along like blind rats in a lab maze. The dab of white from my flashlight struggles to push back the dark. There are light fixtures recessed into the walls, but I can't find a single light switch. The air is stale. By the fifth bend I've lost my sense of direction. All I know is we are moving downwards. Eventually, we see a vertical rectangle of light. It feels like the guiding Bethlehem star, something fixed in a black wilderness.

It's a steel door. I get my knife ready. David turns the handle.

We are at the top of four steps leading down into the garage, which has all its bay doors open. Bob Marley's "One Love" is blasting across a teeming crowd of partygoers. I look at David and see his eyes jumping from person to person; he's equally stunned. At least I'm not the only one feeling like I've just stepped into an alternate universe.

Peter pushes his way through the crowd towards us. "Hey, David, come here," he calls. He's smiling, his eyes twinkling with excitement. David goes over to him. I follow and listen, trying to decide if I should keep David close, as you're told to do with potential enemies, or jettison him immediately? My gut says that as long as he's a McNeil and obeys his brother, I keep him close.

"What do you think? Good idea, hey? I got everyone down here. The whole party, and I mean, everyone! Colleen parked her car across the main gate, jamming the exit. Darren and Grant and their friends are searching the house for Lily and Khetiwe." He gets closer to his brother. "Now you listen up. I called the police. They could close this place down, not let any of us leave. If you want to play in the match tomorrow, you need to get out now. I asked a favour of Aden Hill. He's waiting for you outside the main gate. He drives a lime green Fiat Uno. He'll take you and July home right now."

A getaway car! The one thing I'm trying to prevent. What is Peter's game? He has buckets of influence. Relocating a party proves that, and he has outside people jumping to his whistle. The question is, does he turn a blind eye to crime in favour of keeping a useful connection? I can't trust him. Traitors are always invisible until they strike.

David replies, "Thanks but no thanks. I'm with July. We'll leave when we find Khetiwe and Lily."

Peter scowls and grabs David's arm. "Come, let's talk." He hustles David onto a path that runs next to the garage, away from the watching crowd. David doesn't resist.

Curious to hear the exchange, I get as close to them as I can while remaining unseen.

"Listen-up, shithead!" Peter growls. "Why are you with her? She's not even sane. She does drugs. I saw her this morning passing out from taking something. Look at her! She's a Nobody, a loser. Don't risk your rugby future on her. Go home and let me clean this up."

David pushes Peter's hand off his shoulder. "No, July has her head on straight. She's the only one who does. There's a rapist here. Lily and Khetiwe are missing. We have to find them before he hurts them. I'm with July. She'll find them. Then we all go home."

I take that as my cue and step into the alley. "Hey David— you coming?"

"Yes, I am." He steps past his brother, saying, "We need to check every vehicle here for the girls, even that Uno you have on the outside. I'll tell Grant Wesley about it."

It's a relief to hear he doesn't trust his brother. Maybe we can work together.

Peter drops his voice, "You need to leave. I said you can take her with you."

"What? Walk away when there's work to be done? No. We're finding Khetiwe and Lily. Come with us." Peter shakes his head. David follows me down the path to the rear of the garage.

"I want to check out that bedroom up there." I point to the lighted window above us, to the bedroom that looks out over the garage.

It's a short steep climb. My body fizzes with tension, or it might be the painkillers kicking in, either way I feel lighter, buoyant, able to press on. We reach the door. I check for flashing red lights but see none. Taking a deep breath, I ease the door open. Nothing explodes, yells, or fires. I find a light switch and we get a clear look at the place: a bed, a desk, and a chair all in army-style minimal, clean and neat, except for a pile of clothing up against the fireplace wall.

My heart pounds as I walk towards the clothes. Black denim jeans, a black track top, and brown boots . . . men's boots. I exhale with relief; nothing related to my girls. Then I realize from the angle of the boots that they are still attached to a person lying on the floor. It's not my first dead body, but seeing one again rips away the assumption of existence I walk in and slaps me right up against death, in actual cold detail, here at my feet, as real as the bed in the room, and it bites deeper because tonight I might be just as dead as he is; both of us in the same queue at the Pearly Gates.

"What are you staring at?" David asks walking over to me.

"At him," I point. "He's dead. Help me turn him over. Use your feet not your hands. I want to see who it is." I'm hoping it's one of the Richter gang; one less to attack me or the girls.

David doesn't move. He's turned chalk white. "Dead . . . really? Let's leave. Now! We have to call the police. Shit! I can't be here. I don't want to be included in this mess. My dad will kill me."

His complaining is a good sign, it means he's not about to faint.

"Keep your hair on. Yes, he's dead. If he isn't, he's doing a great job of pretending, and no I can't wait for the police. I have to find the girls before anything happens to them, and looking at this mess, if they were part of it, their survival options just sank to zero." He dithers at the door. I look directly at him, force eye contact. "Come and help me. Let's see who he is." He caves.

It's Andre Vermarck. A pool of blood haloes his head. The blood flows from a gash in his skull. His face is light purple. His mouth is twisted in anger, his eyebrows lifted in surprise. Putting my finger on his jugular I find no heartbeat. David is watching me.

I say, "Yes, he's totally dead."

David makes a gurgling sound and heads into the bathroom to throw up.

Something glitters under the king-size bed. It's a silver hairpin like the ones Khetiwe packed into her fireball hair. I pick it up and a strand of red hair flashes.

"Khetiwe was here," I call to David. "This is her hair and pin."

"Did she kill him?" He says emerging from the bathroom, his face still glistening with sweat.

"He's been maced. That's the purple you see; it marks the attacker so he can be identified. Something surprised him; he stepped back, tripped over the edge of the fireplace, and hit his head on the steel grate." I walk over to the door and open it, thinking I heard something but no one is there. I close it again. "Talking numbers, with him out the picture who is holding the girls? There can't be many more of the inner team left. Richter might be getting his own hands dirty."

"Don't know, don't care," David says. "I want to get out of this room. Please! Let's leave and find the girls. I don't want to be blamed for this guy's death."

"Yes. We need to leave. See that green light behind the door? I wish I'd seen it earlier. They know we're here. Come on! Hurry up! We can't help the girls if we're caught, and if Richter thinks they killed Vermarck he will take it out on them."

Back in the garage, the music is even louder. People are dancing and drinking; the party is here to stay. I go across to the brown van parked on the apron and try to get in; all the doors are locked.

"This van bothers me. I need to check it out." I turn to David, who is watching the dancers, and lean close to his ear. "Can you get this van out of here and park it out of sight, like behind those trees near the fence? There's a spark plug on the workbench over there you can use to smash the window."

"I can drive it no problem," he says, "But can you hotwire it?"

"Yes. No problem." I can see he is no longer surprised. I like that he now knows I am a very capable human, not a caricature or an object. He grabs a spark plug and joins me. "This will make a noise."

"No it won't. If you hadn't noticed it's a little loud in here. No one will hear it."

He slams the spark plug into the van window. The glass explodes sending sharp shiny shards flying. I watch the partygoers; no one turns, as I thought, the stratospheric volume swallowed up the sound of the crash.

Reaching gingerly through the shattered window, he opens the door. "Your chariot awaits." He grins. I think he's beginning to enjoy playing the rebel. All that paternal obedience training vaporized by independent thought.

I twist and fold my already origamied body under the steering wheel, thanking the painkillers for making this possible. "It is basic electronics in these old things—circuits and switches. Find the current. Let it flow." The van rumbles to life within ten seconds, my new record. David climbs into the driver's seat and examines the dashboard, pedals, and hand brake.

While he figures it out, I move into the back of the van. It is stacked high with bags of white powder and small boxes all neatly labeled and organized alphabetically in rows, like in a pharmacy. The girls are not in here. There is no sign of struggle. They've never been in here. This might have been their initial destination, but the gang has been forced to change its plans because I'm eating their zebra one by one.

With a huge crunch and a sound like a bulldozer's blade scrapping across a cement road, David finds reverse, but we don't move. Muttering, he stands on the accelerator pedal and with a sudden heavy jolt the van lumbers backwards. I grab on to a seat to avoid being thrown about like a shoe in a tumble dryer.

"Whoa!" David shouts. "It's like having flat tires." His knuckles are white as he hangs on to the bucking steering wheel.

We bump, like peas on a wild trampoline, out the garage and end up against the security fence.

"Shit parking! Crap driving." I say. "I won't use your taxi next time."

"Best I can do with this lump of scrap metal," he replies, climbing into the back with me. He whistles. "Is this what they packed when we watched them?" He runs his finger delicately over a bag, as if expecting the powder to grab his arm and colonize his mind.

"Some similar combination; the white stuff is, I think, cocaine, but they do trade in all drugs." I hand him four of the smaller white bags. "Push them inside the exhaust, really tight. This stuff is worth a fortune. Richter needs it. He will want the van moved. I want to stop him. Hurry, we still have to find Khetiwe and Lily."

I cut short all the wires under the steering wheel, then open the bonnet and remove the distributor cap. I lob it over the fence and out into the veld.

"You should do shot put, join the athletics team," David says. He is covered head to foot in white powder. I laugh. He looks like a baffled ghost. He sneezes, sending powder flying. I step back to avoid the cocaine cloud.

"Couldn't resist taking a sniff, could you?" I tease. He's dead serious.

"One of the bags exploded." He rubs his eyes with the back of his hands, trying to stop the burning. Noticing the state of his shirt, he brushes at the powder and raises another cloud.

"Will this make me high?" His eyes are already glazed.

"If it doesn't, you better get a refund. You need to wipe your face. The less of this stuff you suck in, the better. Do you have one of your usual huge white tissues? Maybe stop breathing for a bit. You don't want to be high playing rugby tomorrow."

He pulls a bunch of tissues from his pants pocket and wipes his face, whizzing and coughing. I'm half expecting to see a pair of lungs arrive in the next spasm. He looks wobbly.

"Give me your coat." I walk about two metres away and shake it out, turn it inside out and hand it back to him. The night air is cold.

"Come. Let's find you a nice warm basket to hunker down

in. Where's your brother when I need him?" I take his arm and we hobble forward together: the broken and the brain-dead.

"Don't tell Peter. He'll tell my dad. I'm fine. My dad doesn't know I'm here. I have to play tomorrow. I have to. The scouts will be there." He tries to lean on me. I gently push him away. He's bigger than me, heavier, and all my energy reserves are occupied pushing through my own pain and keeping myself upright. He stumbles and looks about to sit down.

"Stay with me, David. Follow my voice. Come, you need to be inside the garage. Just keep walking for about another twenty steps. That's it, now another twenty steps. Almost there."

He's gabbing as he drags himself beside me. "My dad says we have to leave the country because we're white men and South Africa doesn't want us. I guess I can play rugby for New Zealand, but they have their own guys from their own elite schools already in line. They won't need or want foreigners sticking their noses in. If I can't play rugby I don't know what to do . . . "

We reach the garage. Peter is nowhere in sight. I put David on a chair next to the workbench, out of the way. He doesn't need some big mouth telling his dad they saw him high. Finding a tap, I wet a tissue and wipe his face and hands clean like he's my three-year-old in from playing in the mud.

"I'm going to find the girls. You stay here. Okay. Don't move. I'll be back for you."

"No. I'm with you. Why are the stars pulsing red in here? Can you see them?"

"Yes. They are amazing. Watch for the green ones, they're the best. Stay here. Have a snooze. I'll be back in a second."

I move across the driveway, through the entrance gate and up the stairs. In the Great Room, I find Darren Wesley pacing. I approach him, but stay outside grab range.

"Is Lily with you?" he asks.

"No. Time's running out. You know this place, think of a hiding spot."

He runs both his hands through his hair making it stand up like a parrot's crest.

"I've searched everywhere, but if I have to raze it to the ground brick by brick I will." I believe him. His eyes glow with anger; or is it guilt?

"Have you checked all the tunnels and passages in the hill?" I ask. Something flickers in his eyes, just a glimmer; the end of a lightening flash; no power but definitely there. He knows that I know more than he wants me to know. I look away to give him a chance to think. Will he silence me or rescue his sister from his friend? He takes out his phone and issues orders to what sounds like an army.

I leave. I want to examine a certain dumbwaiter.

31. THE POLICE

I CAN'T FIND IT. The dumbwaiter doesn't end in the kitchen. I've even checked in every cupboard to see if they are what I think they are, including the fridge and freezer. Branching out, I move down the corridor closest to the kitchen and find a large utility room. In it are four huge washing machines, two tumble dryers, a box freezer, and an industrial dishwasher. I lock the door behind me and check inside all the machines.

Then I see the cupboard next to the door. I assumed it held all the detergents and cleaners, but inside is a shaft the size of a double wash basket. There are three buttons on the inside wall: up, down and stop. I press the up button and hear the hum of a small motor. Not knowing what will arrive, I get out my knife. A large brown army kit bag appears, chained and padlocked at the top. From its shape I guess there's a person inside. Carefully cutting it open I find Khetiwe, drugged but not bloodied: red hair and silver pins, silver shoes and black bum bag.

I ease her out the bag and on to the floor. The rapist hasn't attacked her yet. Sitting down next to her I whisper,

"Hi Khetiwe. July here. Khetiwe, if you can hear me open your eyes. Khetiwe? Khetiwe, open your eyes."

They flicker a little and then open. She has beautiful amber eyes with flecks of gold. She finds my hand and holds it. "Help Lily. They have Lily. Lily . . . "

"I will. I promise." She falls asleep gripping my hand. I phone Grant and tell him to get here.

He arrives with Darren. They want Lily. I have Khetiwe.

They struggle to hide their disappointment as I say, "She needs to be taken home immediately. They drugged her with a date rape drug. She says the rapist has Lily." I feel wet on my cheeks. "He does terrible things. You have to find your sister."

They exchange glances and Darren runs out of the room.

Grant steps forward. "You also need a doctor. Did he get you? You look like you're in a lot of pain. You shouldn't be running around. Come with me. I'll take Khetiwe down and get you both help." I shake my head.

"No I'm not coming. I must find Lily. Look after Khetiwe."

He's surprised. "Sure? Okay. Do you have her folks' number?" Again, I shake my head. "Directory Inquires it is then." He looks at me. "What do you think is happening to Lily now?"

"Being positive, she's been stashed like Khetiwe until the ruckus dies down. Being negative, after he's raped the girls his gang members dump them someplace out of the way. As no car can get in or out of the parking lot, I think she's either in a tunnel, a bedroom, or a vehicle."

I can see his hands shaking. He lifts up Khetiwe and leaves. As I watch him, a thought strikes me: is Leyton still out on the top lawn? If he isn't, I can follow his blood trail and maybe find the gang's hideout, and Lily.

Up on the lawn, I hear the wail of a siren. Blue lights swoop slowly across the black valley. A lone yellow police van speeds up the dirt road and pulls up close to the blocked gate. A uniformed policeman jumps out. He has a pistol strapped to his hip. I recognize him instantly. He does resemble Darren. Lucas du Toit has arrived home ready to be served his party snacks.

I phone Grant.

"What?" I can hear him panting.

"Just listen, okay? Lucas du Toit is the rapist." He doesn't argue. "He is entering the property right now dressed as a police officer. Find someone to stop him. He must be stopped. Tie him up or lock him up someplace. He is here to rape your sister. You must stop him."

"Thanks, July. Khetiwe is with Colleen and Peter. Got to go."

Leyton Donaldson is not where he fell. His blood travels across the ridge of the yard in the direction of the security fence that surrounds the property. The big square lights above the fence help me follow the blood stains to a steep path running parallel to the fence. About half way down the slope, it turns and heads deeper into the property. Off this path, tucked into the hill, I discover another bedroom. The brother who built this bedroom really wanted privacy.

Ahead of me, I hear shuffling feet, whispers, and a cough. I see Richter and Mpho carrying something wrapped in a blanket. They walk single file along the path. I dial Grant to update him.

Another siren wails across the veld. An ambulance, red and white lights flashing, trundles up the narrow path.

Grant asks, "Did you call for an ambulance?"

"No. It's clever though, using an ambulance as an escape vehicle. Richter knows the van's stuck and people automatically allow an ambulance through. Put it out of action."

"No problem. You get down here. Once we have Lily we're leaving."

"I'm on my way."

I don't see Lucas du Toit, he's disappeared. Once I know Lily is safe, I'll find him.

I follow Richter and Mpho down the path. It turns again and this time stays next to the fence. If we keep going straight down we'll arrive at the main gate and the crowded driveway full of partygoers unable to leave.

By now Richter and Mpho are aware that Grant and at least six more people are tracking them. When they reach the main gate, they stop and dump their bundle on the driveway. The bundle doesn't shift or shout; if it's Lily I hope she is only asleep. When Richter stands up he's holding a pistol and it's pointed at Grant. Everyone drops down, taking cover behind cars and bushes.

Richter shouts, "Back away or I'll kill you."

Holding my hammer tightly in my hand I creep to within a metre of him and Mpho.

"Give us our sister and we'll talk." Darren stands in front of Grant, all lawyer, trained to get his own way.

Mpho sees me and dives off into the bushes; he knows this gang is finished. Richter, focused on Darren, doesn't notice. I glide towards Richter, hammer raised. I'm totally in my body, clearheaded and unafraid.

"I want a getaway vehicle or I will kill your sister."

"We'll talk getaway vehicles once you give us what we want."

I raise my hammer and smash it down on Richter's right hand. With a howl he drops the pistol. In a flying tackle Grant brings him down, gets up and kicks him in the face several times. I offer Grant two plastic ties. He takes them and turns Richter into a trussed chicken. Darren picks up the gun then moves over to the blanket. I help him peel away the blood-soaked woolen cloth. It's Lily. My throat cramps with shock and sorrow. Her face looks pulped like mine. There's blood, lots of it.

Disbelief, fury, and fear swarm across Darren's face. He cradles his sister in his arms then calls, "Grant! Get the car now. Put Khetiwe in. July you get in too, and thank you. We need to get to a hospital." There is a flurry of activity, people eager to wipe this sight from their minds through action. Car engines start, those used as exit obstructions move. The gate opens.

With no one watching Richter I go over to him take out my knife and cut him from below his left eye all the way down to his lip. It's less than he's done to Lily. It'll serve as a warning mark to all women telling them to avoid him. He screams and wiggles. No one looks our way. Wiping my knife on his shirt I return to Lily and her brothers.

Grant arrives with the station wagon. He's folded down the backseats. The boys ease the girls into the back and Erin climbs in next to them. She beckons to me. I shake my head. The boys get in the front. Darren takes the wheel. He opens his window.

"There's space for you in the back. Get in quickly!"

"Don't hassle about me," I say, "I'll find a ride home."

He nods, lets out the clutch, and drives away.

I set off towards the brown van. It is time to find and deal with Lucas du Toit.

32. THE MEETING

"HEY JULY, HAVE YOU SEEN DAVID?" Peter McNeil jogs across to me as I arrive at the garage. My post-fight boxer's face is starting to stiffen, forcing me to talk out of the side of my mouth like a movie gangster.

"Yes. He needs you." I lead him to his brother, who is passed out in the corner where I placed him. At least he's still alive.

"What is wrong with him?" Peter asks, nudging David with the toe of his shoe.

"Not sure. You'll have to ask him. Last thing I knew he was telling me you folk were on your way to New Zealand, joining the chicken run."

Peter's eyebrows shoot up in outrage. "That is private information. He shouldn't have shared it. You don't tell anyone, okay?"

"I might forget if you do me a favour and give me a lift home."

He startles, as if I've demanded a gold carriage and six white horses.

"I'm in Colleen's car. I'll have to ask her and let you know."

"Okay. So it's a maybe on both requests."

He says, "Oh, nearly forgot, Darren said to tell you, if you asked, which you didn't, but whatever, here you are, Lucas du Toit is over near the van."

I'm glad Darren thought to warn me. Peter pulls David to his feet, gets his shoulder under David's arm and drags him, soldier-style, out of the garage.

I circle the Transit van, knife ready, but I don't find Lucas du Toit. Then from a patch of dense bush I hear a groan. If it's a trap I'm already dead meat. No one in my team can help me. I search the bushes. A hooded figure in police blues lies on his side, both his hands and feet are tied and the noose around his neck is fastened to his ankles. If he uncurls he will strangle himself. Black tape covers his mouth. An enraged person did this. My mind jumps to Darren Wesley but I have no way to substantiate my hunch.

Putting away my knife, I take a scarf out of my pocket and mask my nose and mouth. If this doesn't work, I don't want him to identify me. Moving closer, I examine the nails on his pinkie fingers: long and filed into sharp points. At my touch he jerks to life, twisting and groaning. Pulling the canvas bag off his head I examine his eyes: blue, rounded sockets, bulging. This is my rapist. There is no doubt in my mind. He and his followers hurt girls, any girls and all girls because this society lets them. But I will not. My one-person-sized part of South African society says NO!

I am calm. My fingers don't shake, my eyesight remains clear. I worked for this moment, I leaned into it, strived for it, wanted it above all things, and here it lies at my feet, waiting for me. I am ready. My path is bright, straight, and smooth. I check that no one else is around before initiating part one of my secret plan.

He watches me, not expecting any help. He's right. That's not my mission.

I move to make sure he can see me. From my pocket I take a small, narrow, plastic case and a pair of thin medical gloves. Finger by careful finger I slide on the gloves, checking they fit perfectly and sit snugly at my wrists, then I ease open the case and gently remove a bubble wrapped package. As I unwrap this I make sure he can see the syringe full of blood. It isn't.

It's coloured water. I thought about using my own blood but worried it might be traceable in an investigation. Lifting up his light blue police shirt I expose his much-punctured stomach. When he squirms, I know my plan is working. I insert the needle. He strains furiously at his bonds but stops when he needs to breathe; that rope around his throat is my friend.

"AIDS kills so many rape victims," I say, watching the liquid level sink down the vial. "My mother died this week from AIDS; the doctor wrote pneumonia on her death certificate, but that's how it is with AIDS it's so cunning, it lets other illnesses take the blame. Also, there's less stigma if you die from pneumonia instead of AIDS. Did I tell you my mother was a nurse? That's how I got all this stuff and know how to use it." The vial is almost empty.

He gives a violent twist. I let go of the syringe, worried the needle might snap off inside him, another clue that might interest a cop, but again his need to breathe ends his resistance. I continue,

"My body is a gift from my mother. I grew up in it. It is my first possession. It contains my heart, my brain, my essential organs and my thoughts, hopes, dreams, all wrapped up neatly inside my skin. That's epidermis, if you're a nurse. My mom said our bodies are sacred temples. You knifed my skin, you raped my flesh; you meant to kill me, but dying wouldn't just happen to my flesh it would take all of me, my flesh and my mind. I survived, and while my flesh began healing, it turns out my thoughts, witnessing the violation of their home, fled the scene of the crime. They left my body. Homeless, they fixed on two goals: keeping me safe and finding real justice. I won't heal until my thoughts return to my body. They won't return until I build them a safe home. Tonight, now, I lay the first brick." The vial is empty. I remove the needle, place it back in the bubble wrap and lay it gently in the case.

With a wail of sirens several police cars arrive. They have dogs and the dogs are barking furiously. For a drug-sniffing dog this place is heaven. They'll come my way because I'm close to the mother lode in the van. No time to waste, I must start part two of my plan.

Taking a second, fatter syringe full of a murky, white liquid out of the case, I flick it to erase any bubbles then show it to him. His eyes bulge. He blinks. He's scared. He knows what it is. He tries to worm his way out of my reach, twisting like a snake along the ground. I pull on the neck rope. He stops. While cutting me open with his knife, he told me mercy wasn't his style. I won't offend him by offering him any.

"I see you recognized one of your own syringes. You're right, I got it out of your van, from that grey plastic box marked 'specials' that you keep in the cubby. Leyton called it a 'problem fixer.' You probably know that your friend Darren Wesley isn't a friend any more, not since you attacked his sister, Lily. Your gang is broken. Andre Vermarck is dead. What you had is gone. It's over. We know what you did. You're finished and, after that first syringe, you might want one of your own; like comfort food."

I place the needle against his hip, leaving him the choice to roll on it or not. This is my biggest gamble. If he chooses not to, I have a part three because he doesn't get to walk away free from this meeting. I will hand him to the police even if I don't trust their justice.

"Get away from my brother, you bitch!" Leigh-Anne du Toit walks towards me. She points a pistol at my face, her expression twisted with rage.

Is this how I die? I definitely didn't see this coming. I push my scarf down and edge away from Lucas du Toit. She moves closer to him, pushes him with her toe. He doesn't respond.

Behind her two policemen approach with pistols ready. I eye

slide to let her understand they are behind her, and to take her mind off putting a bullet between my eyeballs.

"Hey, lady, this is the police, put down your weapon! Put your weapon on the ground!"

Leigh-Anne decides to follow their orders, bending down and placing her pistol in the ground close to her brother. They handcuff her and one leads her away to the waiting vans.

While they are busy I pocket my case and gloves and stand up. A cop walks over to me.

"Who is this?" he asks looking at du Toit.

"He's Lucas du Toit. It's his house. That girl is his sister."

The cop shines his flashlight at du Toit and sees the uniform. Crouching down, he strips the black tape from Lucas du Toit's mouth and taps du Toit's face. Into his radio he calls, "I need a medic here, immediately. Over near the brown van." He stands up and asks me. "Who tied him up like this?" I shrug and shake my head. He says, "It's a professional job."

Two medics arrive with a bag and a stretcher. They examine Lucas du Toit.

"He's dead, sergeant," one says, putting on gloves to examine the body. He finds the syringe and pulls it out, "Probably this," he lifts it up high then places it into a plastic bag.

The sergeant says, "That makes three dead. Tell the doctor to come here when he finishes with the others. What was going on at this place tonight?" He looks at me. "Who did that to your face?"

I lightly finger the little tapes Khetiwe carefully placed to repair the rip. "A guy flew out of the dark and knocked me down the stairs. I didn't see his face."

"Do you know what happened here?" He points to the house, the partygoers, and the body at our feet.

"She'll know." I point to Leigh-Anne. "She lives here."

"So why are you here? You a friend of hers?"

"We both go to Blue Ridge College. People from the school take turns to offer a Friday night party all through the term."

"This Blue Ridge is a school here in Rivonia? I've never heard of it."

"It's a Pretoria school. The venue is set by the person who provides the party."

"You came all this way alone?" He's looking me up and down.

"I came with friends." We both turn at the sound of someone yelling. It's Peter McNeil.

"Hey, July! Here! Come here! Now! Do you want a lift home or not?"

The sergeant says, "Give your contact details to the corporal here and you can leave."

I take one last look at the corpse of my rapist. My plan has worked. He will never threaten or hurt any girl ever again. I am safe. My eyes have accepted the news, but my brain is busy deactivating all the circuits of fear he created. I can move freely, plot my own path without expecting an attack around every corner.

I limp towards Colleen's car. My body is stiffening from the cold into its broken shapes: twisted hip, lifted shoulder, torn lips.

Looking up at the night sky, I find the four points of the Southern Cross. I feel grounded, solid, strong.

"Mom, are you close? If you can hear me, you don't have to worry about me anymore. I can take care of myself. But, I'd still like to hear from you, when you can. I love you."

A barking police dog has its nose pointed at Colleen's car. I climb into the back seat next to David. His eyes are open and he winks conspiratorially at me and slowly puts his finger to his lips. I shake my head. I'm done with secrets. From my pocket I take four more painkillers and swallow them dry. I hope Mrs Gresham has something stronger in her house.

Colleen lets out the clutch. The car eases forward. She says, "Obviously, July, you need a hospital. What happened to your face? Do you have insurance or some kind of coverage or must I take you to Tshwane District?"

"The person I'm staying with is a nurse. Just take me there." I give her the address and tell Peter. "What's your plan with David? He needs a shower, clean clothes, and landing time before your father sees him."

"What? Why?" Peter cranes his neck around to look at his brother. Now I'm convinced the guy needs glasses, but maybe he won't wear them because they'll spoil his looks.

"That white stuff all over him is cocaine," I explain. "We are all snorting as we drive."

"How the hell did that happen?" Peter asks David. Colleen cracks open her window; road dust joins the pungent mix in the car.

David smiles, gives a thumbs-up and says, "The bag exploded." He starts laughing. Peter gives me a look that could strip the bark off a tree at a hundred paces.

"Where did he get a bag of cocaine?"

"Four!" David says.

"The brown Ford Transit van was stacked with the stuff," I answer.

Peter and Colleen exchange glances. Like everyone at Blue Ridge they knew about the van and Richter and the drugs, but they never said a word, never stood up to expose him, which empowered him to expand, take as much as he wanted, hurt who he wished.

Tonight, I stopped him.

Colleen says, "After we've dropped off July, we can go to my place and get David cleaned up."

David whispers, "Did you hear the dog, hey, July? It didn't

stop barking once; determined to do its job. Lucky for me nobody paid it any attention." He chuckles and passes out.

I lean back, exhausted. I see multicoloured stars. Strangely, my head is silent, like it's taking a well-earned nap. I'm not under threat. It doesn't need to help me think ahead to survive. My body feels light. That heavy backpack dragging me down has disintegrated. This morning I began Part Two of my life and it is already a success. I'm free.

QUESTIONS FOR DISCUSSION

1. Does how you feel about the protagonist, July Abraham, change as you move through the novel?
2. Describe Blue Ridge High School, Pretoria, South Africa as a setting in the novel.
3. The novel is about how rape is still an ever present and real threat to all women in every society. Do you think this might be what maintains sexual inequality across all societies?
4. What do you think motivates July to find and remove the rapist?
5. Why does July include Khetiwe and Lily in her quest?
6. Why does the subject matter suit a first person account?
7. How would you describe the novel's style?
8. Music is part of the fabric of the novel. How did listening to it deepen your experience of the story?